For Betty

1

A group of children waited outside a two-story house that looked identical to all the others around it. The homes continued down the road as far as the eye could see in an unbreaking row. The eager children waited in steadily falling snow. Huddled close together, the kids looked around for their teacher. Their hands laden with books, they started to entertain themselves with the vapor clouds emitting from their mouths.

“Where is he? I’m freezing!” asked Marci.

“I don’t know, I don’t care” exclaimed Crux.

“Ooooo I’m telling!” said Beth.

The children began to bicker amongst themselves. They were a group of seven and all from prominent families in the Harn district of Sagen, the capital of Kreshant. All affluent and used to the privilege of being never left wanting. Mostly spoiled and heavily opinionated with a splash of humility. Their ages ranged from 5 to 11 years. They were present to receive lecture from their most sought-after teacher. One who is renowned for his style, and the success of his disciples. Education of this caliber was only available to those with high positions and deep pockets. This day their mysterious teacher was running late.

“I see him! Over there!”

“You idiot, that’s a cow.”

“Ooooo I’m telling!”

“Shut your mouth Amon!”

A tall looming figure appeared behind the children, dark and imposing. The kids all turned and gasped.

"Good Morning my students." There he stood, the mysterious teacher they were all freezing for. He was at least 6ft tall and was very wide in the waist area. He too held books in his mittened hands and seemed toasty in his thick tunic, bulky trousers, and huge leather boots. The children's eyes all fixed on his face, or lack of one. All they saw was a white smiling mask with red borders around sausage shaped eye and mouth holes. He had thick, long, and messy hair that reached towards the sky and down his back almost touching his boots.

"Welcome." He turned to the door and stuck in a large heavy iron key. The thick wooden door swung open with a loud creak revealing the cozy home with a warm fireplace to soothe ice cold bodies. The students shuffled in, rubbing their hands together and rubbing the sides of their arms. An instant pile of mittens, coats, scarves and other items blocked the entrance. The teacher gently kicked the clothing out of the way and closed the door, barring the eager cold from getting in.

The kids were being loud and blurting all kinds of nonsense about their families' riches, toys, games they liked to play and other things. They huddled in a mass at the fireplace which crackled and popped as they warmed up.

"Children, now that you have made yourselves comfortable please come to the rug and take a seat. Most of the group of four boys and two girls ignored the order and continued to warm themselves. One girl named Maya, the youngest, about 5 or 6 looked back at him and then gave her attention back to the flames.

"I will not ask again, you either come now, or back outside you go." The light from the fireplace suddenly dimmed, and then returned to its regular brilliance. They all contemplated the threat. Would he really do this knowing the repercussions that their affluent names would unleash upon him. The children all stared at their teacher. The lifeless holes in the mask stared back at them. He was motionless, soundless, and seemingly, soulless.

A light growling sound began to leave his mask. One by one they slowly walked to the thick shaggy rug that was laid out before them, about 15ft in diameter. Some tried not to stare at his face and quickly looked away, others stared the whole way from the fireplace to the rug. Once seated, they remained quiet as the statuesque figure holding its pose. A low voice crept out the mouth hole of the mask.

"Now that we are all settled in; we may begin the lecture." his voice then returned to normal and the home felt alive and bustling again.

"I am your teacher. They call me Stosay, for I am a story sayer." He reached to the shelf behind him and pulled out a large book. It was as thick as a man's fist and the size of a small table. The imposing figure had no trouble with the instrument of learning due to his immense frame. Marci, the other little girl in the group stared at Stosay with a perplexed look on her face. She just could not continue until she knew the reason he was wearing that ridiculously mask.

"Are you going to ask him about the mask?" asked Maya who sat right next to her.

"No. why don't you ask him?"

"You're afraid, aren't you?" teased Maya.

"I am not." Marci was getting angry as Maya who was 2 years younger covered her mouth and softly giggled.

"I'll do it." Exclaimed the voice of Crux, one of the four boys and by far the most outspoken of the students.

"You'll do what?" Stosay's voice pierced the air and grabbed the young boy by his very soul. Usually confident he stammered and tried to piece together a sentence explaining his exclamation.

"I...um... was just telling... they were... I was just."

"Why do you wear mask?" blurted little Maya. She covered her mouth and opened her eyes as wide as they could go. The others gasped in horror as they awaited Stosay's reply. All eyes fixed on him and he froze once again. His dead stare was very intense. The mask, though smiling, gave a sinister vibe that could be very unsettling.

"A valid question my little, Maya is it?" Maya then let out a grin that showed her relief as did the rest of the class.

"My form is horribly disfigured. I was made this way by the gods. All that, along with wars and sicknesses, made me dawn this mask to hide my true form." Another question was about to be asked when Stosay cut it off quickly and began the lesson.

"Children please leave your questions for the end of the lesson." A quick glance was made left to right with the empty black eyes. The children sat quietly and gave their attention to their teacher. Stosay opened the huge book titled, *The History of Boe Chantra*, and turned it to the final chapter.

"Let us begin."

Loss Of The Enchantrics

The God of the dead was a highly disgruntled and loathsome being. He sat on a throne comprised of thousands of damned souls. The worst of the worst were there, moaning and groaning for an absolution that would never come. These souls were the heaviest among the rest, such was their burden and guilt that they were too heavy to rise to the heavens. So they festered like a putrid carcasses in the plains of sorrow. Bazetar, on the other hand, could leave his realm whenever he wanted. Unlike them, he was not a mortal and did not possess a soul. He could go and relax with other prime gods like Aires, god of war, Acuas, god of water, Relo, storm god, Yarmas, fire god, Teras, god of land, or even the lord of all, Attel. He lived a comfortable and privileged life, wielding amazing power.

Still the countless boring eons passed, taking an immense toll on his mind. He desired his own kingdom to rule over. A rich living land away from the dead and away from his kin who seemed content with what they had. All was good, but then again it was not. He devised a clever plan. He would renounce his title as lord of the Plains of Sorrow and live amongst the living as their new ruler. A living deity in their midst. In his resignation he would lose a significant portion of his power, but would gain a soul giving him rich emotional sensations. This was something he had already considered and was just fine with. He would steal the urn of the first lord, the shapeless one. There resided part of the original ruler of all the lands. The being was trapped in an eternal jail from which only half of it was entombed; the other was lost to time. Bazetar went to work and quickly as his scheme began to bear fruit. He stole the urn from under the noses of Attel's guards for there was no reason to suspect any turmoil. Once in his possession he opened the urn and out stretched a matte black goo. The tip of the goo took the form of a clawed hand and grabbed Bazetar's wrist. In one motion it enveloped the lord of the dead and he felt an ecstasy for which there is no comparison. Bazetar instantly transformed and grew two feet measuring 8 in all. Power surged through his body making him toned, and muscular. His hands which had numbered 5 digits were reduced to three. From his forehead sprouted five long points taking the shape of a of brow crown. Now Bazetar, the lord of the dead had become the Troll King.

Once found out, much was done to try to stop him, but it was all in vain. He now had his power amplified greatly and even the great Attel tried to intervene, but failed. In a great cacophony of light and magic Bazetar made his great escape into the world of mortals. He was given a soul as he fell and descended on humanity in the country of Bole Va.

It was a country vastly unprepared to deal with an invasion. Bazetar used his knowledge of the evil arts to create an army made up of gray beings that were almost a mirror image of himself except for their size. They were the height of a normal human and he named them, "The Trowcans." Each Trowcan was given the soul of a damned resident of the Plains of sorrow, allowing Bazetar to create them by the thousands. From a black portal he raised from nothing they marched out by the hundreds of thousands. No army was a match for their ferocity and general lack of empathy or fear. The souls that now possessed bodies were more than happy to attack the living to seek retribution for their own follies. Bazetar would purposely starve them before a battle so that they would consume the enemy's flesh to create panic.

After Bole Va was left void of inhabitants, Bazetar turned his attention to the neighboring country of Kreshant. Unlike Bole Va; Kreshant had a standing army that was renowned for its bravery and discipline in battle. This would not be an easy victory so the Troll King doubled his forces. If he could take this country, all the rest on the continent of Boe Chantra would fall easily.

On a dark gloomy day, there stood an army that blocked the path of this immense horror. The Trowcans had arrived. The Trowcan army ravaged the land, killing all the living without mercy. Their advance to the south put them on a collision course with the powerful and prosperous land ruled by King Crenon of Kreshant. His highly trained army of knights, archers, spearmen, cavalry, and many lesser skilled volunteers thirsted for glory. It was a force of which was never seen before. They could have certainly conquered a huge chunk of the continent and held with ease if they so chose.

As seen from above, a huge gray mass marched towards Crenon's army which was blocking the road leading to the Castillo Morta. The Castillo Morta was the gigantic castle that sat atop a plateau inside a deep crater. It had one causeway leading in from the rim of the crater to the enormous gatehouse plaza. As the Trowcan army arrived they looked at the castle with awe and amazement as the castle easily dwarfed all others. Crenon glared at the opposing army that halted 500 yards away from his position. He studied the Trowcans and realized that the reports that stated they were just a mindless mass of bodies were untrue. He noticed formations of foot soldiers that made up the bulk of their numbers. Each warrior held a wooden circle shield and a curved slashing sword with light armor. The Trowcans also had a regiment of cavalry riding dark hog like beasts the size of a horse.

Crenon turned away, put his hands on his hips and sighed looking at the dry ground at his feet.

"What troubles you father?" asked a 12 year old Heron with a concerned look on his face.

"I fear the Trowcans will overrun us." Crenon stared at his boy with great love and sadness knowing that this could be their last day together.

"Father, surely all hope is not lost. We can escape to the castle. We can even make our way to the outer island till the threat goes away." Young Heron gave other options but Crenon knew that this Trowcan menace had to be dealt with here for it would not stop till all natural life was extinguished. He let out a slight grin and placed both hands on his child's armored shoulders.

"Son, we are the Sagen family. Our lineage has governed our people for ages. Many challenges have befallen our ancestors and they have always risen to the occasion, as must we. Fear not my son, it is okay to worry during dire times but keeping a calm head during those situations. That is what makes you a Sagen." Heron thought about what his father said and cringed at his show of cowardice. He unsheathed his sword and exclaimed, "To the death father!" Crenon smiled and proudly hugged his boy with his left arm still keeping his right on the hilt of his sword.

"All hail the great Sagen King!" exclaimed a female voice from above.

"Elsia?" inquired Crenon as he squinted to focus on the winged being.

"It is you! My friend! Though I delight in your presence, I fear this place is too dangerous for you."

"My King, we the Enchantric people hold an oath to these lands. They will always be under our protection. We meet any danger to the people of Boe Chantra. We wish to join your ranks so that we may help undo this threat and return these lands to peace." Crenon looked at the scantily clad Elsia. She was beautiful with supple curves and with a soft glow to her skin. Her crimson wings moved slowly back and forth keeping her stationary in the air. She was the queen of the Enchantrics, a race of magical beings put on Boe Chantra by the supreme god Attel to watch over the continent. Over time, the misuse of their powers and talents by greedy warlords saw their numbers dwindle to an even thousand, who were all present on this day.

"My beloved queen, I reluctantly accept your assistance. I would prefer you and your people leave and seek refuge, but I cannot help but feel a pinch of relief seeing you here. Perhaps you are what we need to tip the balance of battle."

"Please Crenon, command us. Give us our positions."

"Yes my queen. Stretch your forces along the length of our line. We will need your power covering us from above."

"It will be done Crenon." She turned quickly and looked at Isd, her longtime lover and captain, "You heard the king. Order all to their positions."

"As you wish my queen. Enchantrics! Fly!" The sky was cluttered with movement as a thousand winged beings moved to their stations. Crenon was going to address his own captains when another voice called out.

"My king we have arrived to assist you!" Crenon looked and saw a group of soldiers from the country of Brethen Paya. They were heavily armored and bore the crest of their king on their gold adorned shields.

"Brethen Paya has arrived! Is that all of them?" shouted a knight of Kreshant. His sounded nervous as the king gave him a disapproving stare.

"So, you are my reinforcements promised by your king?" asked Crenon.

“Yes sire.” Answered the leader of the king’s guard.

“It seems many of you are on leave at the moment. I was promised many more soldiers.”

“Apologies my great king. We are only the king’s guard. Our lord was overruled by our senate, so he sent us in their place. Worry not my king. We are fierce fighters, and will continue to battle till the very life is beaten from our corpses.” He knelt before Crenon pledging his loyalty to him.

“Rise Payan. I appreciate you coming to help us. What is your name?”

“I am Prince Tetso, son of King Lornet.” Crenon raised his eyebrows trying to process what he had just heard.

“Please take position in the center.” Was all he could muster.

“Yes my lord. Let’s go men!” The king’s guard marched with machine like movements to the center of Crenon’s line. Crenon wanted the most skilled and heavily armored infantry in the middle so that they could absorb the coming charge. Crenon’s own knights were well armored, but did not compare in skill or caliber to the Payans.

“Father, they are too few to add significant strength to our army.”

“Yes my son, they are only about 5,000.” Heron’s eyes widened.

“Still they are the guards of the king accompanied by his son. That means that they are the best of the best Brethen Paya has to offer. Sending them to us was an great sacrifice for the king. It’s a sign of great respect and having such great warriors at our side will boost morale.”

A loud chant began to echo on the battlefield. It was loud and rhythmic. Weapons kept pounding the ground, shaking the earth. The Trowcans were getting restless and their excitement spread throughout their ranks. Their piercing, glowing yellow eyes were fixed on the opposing army, with cat-like pupils. The chant continued unintelligibly and many of Crenon's soldier felt a chill go up their spines. All had heard the stories coming from Bole Va's refugees. Tales of entire prosperous cities wiped out in mere days. There were also reports of babies and children being roasted over fires and consumed as great delicacies amongst Trowcan officers.

A lone soldier in Crenon's army began to lose his nerve. Sweat engulfed his body and his armor made him feel trapped and unable to breathe. He shook profusely while trying to maintain his stance. His fellow knights turned and asked if he was fine, but the soldier, now going mad with anxiety, did not answer.

"They're going to eat us!" He burst out in a fit of panic, broke ranks and ran wildly onto the battlefield. The soldier ripped off his helmet gasping for air. He fixed his wild eyes on the Trowcan army. He began to whimper in complete madness.

"Do you not see men? This king of ours has led us to our doom! You'll all be in the bellies of those monsters tonight!"

"Control yourself man! That is your king!" a knight grabbed him from behind as another tried to restrain him from the front. The crazed soldier broke a hand loose striking the soldier in front breaking his nose. Then he turned with his unsheathed sword and stabbed the one behind driving the blade into his shoulder. The injured soldier fell to the floor writhing in pain.

"I curse you Sagen King! I curse you to the Plains of Sorrow!" the bewildered soldier ran aimlessly, engulfed in his own lunacy. After running for a while he tired and faced his king. With sword in hand he continued to curse and rant. A large shadow suddenly engulfed him. He felt a hot stinking breath on his neck followed by a low rumbling growl. A terrible, almost painful chill crawled up his spine as he slowly turned to look at the ferocious Sav Trow behind him. It stood nine feet tall with arms and legs as thick as the trunk of an old tree. It stood there clad in thick, heavy armor and holding an axe which would be impossible for a human to wield. Deep in its horned helmet were two glowing orbs for eyes. Suddenly it let out a loud roar that shook the battlefield and made the soldier scream in a high pitch. The massive axe rose in the air above the Sav Trow's head and came down cleaving the man in two. His torso fell to the ground and the Sav Trow sat and pulled his warm entrails to its hungry mouth. Life left the soldier as his soul went to be judged by Helgon, the dragon of judgment. Many other Trowcans began to break ranks to view the beast relish his feast, but none dared approach. A Sav Trow would just as likely make a Trowcan into a meal as it would a human. Only the most evil souls were personally chosen by Bazetar to take this form.

"Your subjects break ranks my lord," said a soft spoken voice, "perhaps it is time to unleash this horde on the humans. Kragnus, Bazetar's supreme general, studied his face waiting for a response as his king stared at the human army.

"These mortals defy me. Many of them commit horrible crimes. Great evil is in their nature and yet they stand in my way. After today's battle, many of them will join me." Bazetar turned to his general and pointed at the enemy with his left, three fingered claw. "Sound the charge. Let us get this army fed." Kragnus was abnormally taller than the rest of the uniformly 5ft 9in Trowcans and stood a good 6ft 2in. The left side of his upper lip was always raised slightly revealing his sharp teeth. Kragnus turned to his captains and gave them a shallow nod. In unison multiple horns blared, loudly filling every crevice of space around the army. "Charge and be fed!" yelled Kragnus while gesturing his claw at the humans. The Trowcans sprinted towards their coming buffet, kicking up a massive cloud of dust that could be seen from the Eagle's Lookout.

Matiun, King Crenon's younger cousin rushed up to the Eagle's Lookout. It was the highest, and slimmest tower of the Castillo Morta and almost looked like a flagpole from far away. Once he reached the top, he was greeted by a heavy wooden double door which he flung open and shut as he rushed to the edge of the battlements. The echoes of the Trowcan battle horns still blared as he looked down on the battlefield. All he could see was a line of his countrymen facing a gray mass rushing towards them. He reached in his pocket and pulled out a gold lined telescope which he extended and brought to the framed lens of his right eye.

At first, he saw nothing as he moved his telescope around to find the action. He saw the wall of men bracing for collision. He moved around frantically looking for his cousin.

"There you are Crenon. I told you to just hold up in the castle but no... ever the stubborn fool you were when we were children. You always had to have everything your way. Now the devils charge and you leave me with a token force to face whatever horror you will be unable to defeat?" He quickly gave a glance around to see if anyone was around to hear his words of defiance. Of course there was no one, the Eagle's Lookout was empty when he entered it, and if anyone went up there, the sound of the heavy door would've been extremely loud. He looked on, studying the formations of the enemy, gauging their strengths and weaknesses. He noticed that the common Trowcan had light armor, which was a good thing when it came to the castle defenses. He could easily kill thousands of them before they would even make it to the walls. Still, even if the thousands were killed by Crenon and himself, the remaining amount would still be enough to lay siege to the castle ten times over. He wished he was at home with his wife and kids who had long been placed in the soft vaults of the castle meant for the non-combatants and small children. He wished Crenon had not placed him in charge of the castle defenses. Though he was the most qualified for the job, he was very timid and introverted. Quickly he looked to the walls of the castle to make sure every swordsman, pike man, and archer were where they needed to be. He heard a noise like the sound of sea foam bubbles popping. It was very light and distant but he knew it was the sounds of battle. The Trowcan wave was about to crash on the Kreshant army's shore. He kept looking through his telescope, looking for the dreaded Bazetar. Slowly he moved his gaze through the moving clutter of bodies until he came to a figure that was unmistakably god-like in nature. It was he, the scourge of the mortals. He would see them all dead and converted to Trowcans. The beast towered above all the others around him and strode with a confidence that was lacking in most mortals. He was invincible on the mortal plain and his power was overwhelming. As Matiun reviewed Bazetar, he noticed that the God of the Dead had stopped in his tracks and stood still as all the Trowcans rushed around him. Bazetar lifted his head and gazed directly at Matiun staring deep into his soul, over a great distance and through his telescope. Matiun felt a cold chill run up his spine and then he saw and even heard Bazetar say, "Matiun." He cried out in a panicked yelp and fumbled around trying to catch his scope as it fell all the way to the base of the Eagle's lookout. Suddenly there was a loud bang and Matiun cried out again.

"My lord, the Trowcans move!" reported Matiun's personal

guard.

"I see that!" scolded Matiun to the confused guard. "Don't ever sneak up on me like that." He took long deep breaths and had his hand on his heart as he tried to calm down.

"Apologies my lord, I didn't mean to....."

"Worry not my friend. It's not your fault. Please forgive my temper and relay this. All the castle's forces must be at the ready. No excuses, only children and disabled may take refuge in the soft vaults. No one else." He hated himself for saying that. He knew his wife was abled but would not participate in the coming combat. The soldier popped to a salute and ran off the pass on the order. Matiun followed close behind but stopped at the door's entrance.

"My dear cousin, you face a horror worse that any ever seen before. May the gods favor you this day. May you save us all." He left the Eagle's lookout and vanished into The Castillo Morta.

"Release Arrows!" was commanded by Crenon quickly echoed by his captains. A huge battalion of women archers flooded the sky with arrows aimed at the Trowcans.

"Fire on the demons my people!" commanded Elsia from the air as a volley of energy spheres the size of grapefruits were launched by every Enchantric. Many Trowcans were impaled or blown up by the rain of missiles and magic bombs. Those hit by arrows were reduced to a bloody smear on the ground by the thousands of stampeding feet. Those hit by the magic spheres ignited, and were reduced to ashes in an instant. Thousands died and yet the charge continued unabated.

"Brace yourselves!" yelled Crenon, and then there was a deafening sound as the Trowcans crashed the full weight of their army into the shield wall. The Trowcans were excellent jumpers and many were able to leap over the spears and land behind the lines creating panic. The Trowcans began to broadcast their ferocity by killing people, prying open their armor, reaching in with their claws and ripping chunks of warm bloody flesh to consume.

Death was all around. The discipline of the mortals was superior, and they overcame the initial panic and began to work together. Defensive formations held together, and frantic commands were given to maintain the integrity of the army. The Enchantrics continued their aerial bombardment, and along with the constant volley of arrows began to softened the Trowcan onslaught as the humans began to push back.

"My queen! My love! Soon we will have victory!" exclaimed Isd.

"Yes! It appears the mortals may prevail!"

A short distance away, Kragnus observed the carnage. He was appalled by how many had already been lost, and though they still had the numbers, the situation was turning dire. He turned to his forces showing his teeth on the side and yelled.

"These men are nothing more than organized meat! All you have to do is work a little harder for your meal! Nothing more! Advance and overwhelm them!" Kragnus grabbed a spear that was stuck in a knight's back.

"Don't fear the flying insects protecting them!" In a quick motion he launched the spear and it found its mark. It pierced the energy ball that Isd was holding in his right hand and then pierced his torso and only stopped when the tip was blocked by his spine.

"No!" cried Elsia as the energy ball became unstable and in a bright explosion her lover was no more. The remains of his charred corpse plummeted to the ground where they vanished into the chaos of battle. Elsia quickly resumed launching her bombs at the Trowcans. She thought to herself that if they survived there would be plenty of time to mourn later. Her eyes were full of tears but she grit her teeth and continued the fight.

Kragnus continued inspiring the troops to great effect. The Trowcans became more ferocious and began to slowly push the mortal lines back. Kragnus was still concerned for their losses, but his did not make him panic or nervous at all. Kragnus always kept a cool head and never lost his composure, even in the face of impending defeat. He casually strode towards Bazetar to let him know the current state of the army. They would be defeated unless something was done quickly.

"My lord?"

"Speak general."

"We have gained momentum, but it will not last long. We are fast losing bodies, and we still have the coming siege of the castle to prepare for." Bazetar standing two feet taller than Kragnus stared at the armies with his white clouded eyes.

"You have to admire the humans in their attempt at defiance. Even though we hold the advantage of superior numbers, it pales in comparison to those fighting for their lives and their loved ones. I find it very interesting." Bazetar said in a deep and soft voice knowing that Kragnus was listening but not really caring if he was.

"Sire?" Kragnus noticed that Bazetar was silent and didn't move. The former God of the Dead stared off into space.

"My Lord? I think we... If you could just give us an order or..."

"Still, they are dogs. This Sagen king dare think himself

my equal?" his voice began to grow louder.

"If something must be done about these cattle then let it be done!" Bazetar lifted his claw and pointed it towards the human lines. His eyes began to pulse from white to black. A growing surging sound was all around him as his claw lit with a black flowing energy. In an instant the power left his claw at blinding speed and crashed into the mass of soldiers, mortal and Trowcan. The following explosion sent many mangled and burning bodies into the air. Some even hundreds of feet where they almost crashed into the Enchantrics above. The scorched ground sizzled with an intense heat where the black energy had struck.

"What was that?" Crenon frantically asked his captain.

"My lord, the Troll King is moving!"

"Where?"

"Towards us!" said the captain with bulging eyes looking into Crenon's. Crenon noticed that the men were beginning to fall back even more now that Bazetar was now engaging in the battle. He looked around at his men and then to his son.

"I must join the fray." Said Crenon

"What? Father... no. You can't just leave me here. What will I do?" Heron said with great angst for being left alone.

"Calm yourself my son. I need to rally our forces. They are teetering on collapse" Heron ran to his father who was mounting his horse.

"Don't go father. Please! I don't know what to do without you here."

"Don't worry my boy. You'll be fine. Stay here and let the royal guard do their job." Crenon turned his horse towards the fighting and commanded his guard of 20 soldiers to protect the boy at all costs. He rode off and joined his soldiers.

"Come soldiers of Kreshant! Rally to me! Rally to me!" Crenon swung his sword at the Trowcans lobbing off heads, and splitting skulls.

"We are it! We are the wall! And we're not coming down!" the men around him shouted in agreement and resumed the dispatching of the Trowcans. The moral of the mortals was electrified and spread through their ranks as they saw that their king was on the front lines just like they were.

Elsia looked from above at the mortals' reinvigoration and then took her own action.

"Enchantrics! Listen to your queen! The mortals are rallying and now we must do the same! We must unify our power and focus it all on the Troll King!" Instead of firing orbs of energy, the Enchantrics began firing steady beams of glowing light at the advancing Bazetar. Each fired two beams, one from each arm and focused them on Bazetar's chest. Bazetar stopped in mid stride and let out a mighty roar as the shock from the beams spread throughout his massive body.

"Simple parlor tricks are not enough to stop the God of the Dead!" Cocooned in an extremely bright pulsing ball of energy and magic he continued his walk.

"He's walking toward the King!" cried out Elsia.

"He must be stopped!" Elsia tensed all her muscles and squinted her eyes as all the beams grew in intensity. As Bazetar advanced, pieces of fabric from his cape began to flake off as did pieces of skin. The pieces floated in the direction opposite the firing Enchantrics and vaporized, still Bazetar advanced. He was determined not to be stopped.

Heron stood still watching the slaughter of countless lives. Little by little he noticed that the gray of the Trowcan army seemed to get closer and closer. This made him nervous and the fear grew stronger and crippling.

"Guard are we okay?" asked Heron nervously.

"My prince, I'd take cover and stay low if I were you. They'll be among us soon." The guards formed a wall between Heron and the approaching Trowcans. The monsters halted their advance for a second to smile and chuckle at the defenders. Heron was able to get a glimpse of their eyes. They were larger than a human's and yellow. Also, they glowed and were surrounded by some black lines. They trailed up and down their faces. Their laugh break was over and the guards were soon enveloped in battle, oblivious to the state of the prince. Heron ducked behind a baggage wagon he had overturned and looked on at the brave men defending him.

"Well hello down there." Came an eerie voice from Heron's right side. Slowly he turned his head and to his horror he was gazing upon a blood splattered Trowcan holding a wooden shield and a dripping sword. He smiled at Heron with fresh pieces of meat stuck in his bloody teeth.

"Who would leave such a tasty morsel all by himself?" In a quick motion the Trowcan hit Heron's face with the wide part of his circle shield and then butted his head with the handle of his sword. Heron fell on all fours with his eyes completely shut, trying to gather his senses.

"Do you know who I am Prince Heron? I remember when you were just a baby and the whole of Kreshant was a buzz with news of your birth. Oh how the gossip spread. Were you going to be another great ruler like your dad? Were you going to be a ladies' man? It made me sick to my stomach." The Trowcan raised his voice and gave Heron a vicious kick to his stomach.

"I was once human, just like you. I was an assassin for hire. The country, even the whole of Boe Chantra probably knew me as the Red Hand. Have you ever heard of me?" Heron was still grunting in pain while holding his mid-section. The Trowcan used his index claw to pull up Heron's chin to look into his eyes.

"Well? Have you?" he paused for a moment, "Of course not." He let go of Heron's chin and walked a full circle around him.

"I was in my prime. I was amassing unimaginable wealth. I was somebody. Then your father ordered my arrest and after and unfair trial I was sentenced to die for my talent. I was sent to the chopping block and had my head removed from my body. All I remember was a quick sharp pain on my neck and then I was in line to go before Helgon. The judgment dragon quickly told me all my faults, sins, and that my soul was too heavy with evil and malice to remain with the gods. So, the very bridge beneath me was opened and I plummeted to the ground and pierced through it all the way to the Plains of Sorrow. It's a horrible place. No one should ever be sent there regardless of their crimes. I rotted there for many years, slowly going mad. Your father caused all that and now that the great Bazetar has revived me, I will take my revenge... on you!" he grabbed Heron by his hair lifted him to where his knees were above the ground but there was no weight on his feet. Heron held on to the Red Hand's muscular arm to try to get the pressure off his scalp. He felt the Trowcan's blade caress the skin on his throat and also the hot breath on the side of his face as the Trowcan continued to speak.

"I've had my fill of meat for today, but I will make an exception for you my prince." He stuck his clawed finger in his throat and vomited chunks of human meat covered in the smell of stomach acid.

"Now, the barrel is ready to receive its sustenance."

"Heron!" cried out a voice from the mass of bodies. Heron painfully focused on it and saw that it was his father galloping towards him.

"Well, well, well. This is going to get very interesting." Whispered the Trowcan.

"Unhand my son monster!"

"Crenon! How happy I am to make your acquaintance. I am the ghost of the Red Hand, at your service."

"I care not who you are, just release the boy." Crenon dismounted his horse with his bloody sword in hand.

"Sorry but I have a new king that gives me orders and my orders are to slay all you mortals."

"I remember you, a murderer, a great sinner. You were already dealt with once; I will deal with you again!" Crenon brought his sword to the ready. In a blind rage, the Red Hand kicked Heron in the back and sent him flying forward as he rushed towards Crenon. Crenon also ran towards the Trowcan and their swords met in a clash. They were face to face for a brief moment and then the Trowcan's face was met by the back of Crenon's fist. In a daze his first reaction was to raise his shield to protect himself but Crenon had already lifted his sword high above his head and brought it down on the Trowcan's shield. The wooden shield came undone as splinters flew in all directions. The Trowcan barely had enough time to take in what had happened when Crenon's blade was already swiping back in the direction of his neck. The Trowcan ducked, but the blade was able to clip off the tops of his pointy ears which stuck out past the top of his head. As soon as Crenon's sword stopped again it was in motion headed back at the Red Hand who was able to stop it this time with his sword. He then used his bulk to hit Crenon with his shoulder and knock him on his back. He stood over Crenon with an evil smile.

"This is exactly how I dreamed I'd have you. There is no way you could imagine how your state of mind deteriorates as your soul withers in the Plains of Sorrow. I was rotting! You hear me? Rotting! And now here I am! Back and ready to help my lord destroy all you mortals, as well as the gods!" The Trowcan put both hands on his downward pointing sword. He raised it above his head, ready to impale the Sagen King.

"Goodbye mortal king. I hope you get to experience all the horror I had to go through." The Trowcan's blade came down but stabbed only ground as Crenon rolled to his right at the last second. He met the Trowcan again with a metal gauntlet to the face. The Red Hand fell to the ground without his sword and Crenon staggered to his feet ready to finish this fight. He had completely forgotten about the battle raging around him and did not see that there was another Trowcan who had him in its sights. There was a sudden sharp pain in his abdomen. He looked down at his torso and saw the point of a spear sticking out. In one quick motion he spun to his right and slashed his other attacker across the chest, killing him. The spinning motion broke the spear and only a small part stuck out his back. He fell to his knees holding his wound, blood gushing over his golden armor. His hand weakly held his sword. He tried to stay as still as possible because any little movement sent agonizing pain through his body.

"Hello mortal king." the Red Hand now stood in front of the wounded Crenon. He knelt in front of the king and held his chin as he had done to Heron.

"I will suck the marrow from your bones and rip out your son's intestines while he still breathes. But before the festivities, I have this gift for you." With a large serrated knife, the Trowcan stabbed Crenon in the stomach and Crenon let out a cry of pain. He weakly put his hand on the Trowcan's claw trying to keep him from stabbing him again. The Trowcan stood up and chuckled as he saw the blood pooling around the King of Kreshant.

"Behold great Sagen King. It was I, the Red Hand, that bested you. Even after death, I always get my mark!" he let out a loud hearty laugh as he wallowed in his savory revenge. Suddenly a shiny blade came down and split his head all the way to the bridge of his nose. His glowing yellow eyes rolled back into his head and he fell to the ground. The Red Hand was dead once again. Crenon looked up slowly and saw the sword sticking out of the Trowcan's head then he saw Heron standing over him with a bloody beaten face mixed with sweat, dirt and tears. Heron grabbed his father's arm and helped him to his feet. Crenon grunted in pain but amazingly was able to stand.

"I fear I am undone my boy. Those beasts have mortally wounded me."

"Crenon! He approaches! We can't stop him!" cried out Elsia as the combined power of the Enchantrics pounded Bazetar. He still walked towards Crenon as parts of his skin had completely flaked off showing only red bloody muscle all over his body. As the Enchantrics used up their power they began to wither to skin and bone. Their wings began coming apart and in a puff of white smoke they began disappearing once all was depleted. Elsia looked around in horror as the last of her people began to vanish. People she had known for thousands of years since Attel placed them on Boe Chantra to aid the mortals.

"My Queen!" poof! Another Enchantric withered and disappeared. Bazetar was almost upon Crenon when the last 2 left of his royal guard ran to the king's aid.

"Protect the king! Protect the prince!" cried out one guard as he stood in a defensive position. The hideously scarred and glowing Bazetar stood before the guards. He was still surrounded by Elsia's magic even though the rest of the Enchantrics were gone. One of the guards lifted his sword preparing to strike at Bazetar but was quickly impaled by Bazetar's clawed fingers which were almost the length of a child's arms. He lifted the guard into the air and cast his lifeless body aside like an old rag. The other looked in horror as the God of the Dead reached for him, picked him up over his head with both arms, and ripped him in two pieces. Bazetar let out a enfeebled grunt and then fell to his knees. He was weakening and was in great pain. With his power being drain by Elsia's onslaught he could not regenerate fast enough. He rose again to his feet and faced the Sagen King.

"Crenon." Bazetar spoke weakly. He wrapped the fingers of one claw around Crenon and lifted him to eye level.

"Your time is up King of the mortals. I am the new..." Bazetar started buckling under the weight of his wounds.

"I see you're not feeling well Bazetar." Crenon grunted as he adjusted himself inside Bazetar's weakening grip.

"Do you know who I am? I am Crenon, king of the free people of Kreshant and defender of life and prosperity." Crenon lifted his free arm still holding his sword and set it ready to stab. "Now back to the Plains of Sorrow with you!" He then thrust his sword deep into Bazetar's thick muscular neck. Bazetar quickly recovered from his wound induced daze and let out a great roar of pain that shook all who were in his close proximity. In a quick motion, Bazetar angrily raised Crenon into the air and threw him to the ground like a ragdoll. Crenon hit the ground hard and was able to hear his bones snap before blacking out. Heron watched his father's limp body hit the ground and then bounce up a few inches before becoming still. Heron's wide eyes were filled with tears and horror as he felt his innocence leave him forever. The tall dark figure of Bazetar stood before his short and skinny frame with his father's sword still stuck in his neck and gushing blood. He let out a weak whimper as the God of the Dead leaned forward reaching for him with the opposite claw that had taken his father.

"Heron." Said Bazetar in a deep and weak tone. His claw was inches from Heron's face and then the great fallen god fell to his knees. His head hung limply on his shoulders as a steady stream of drool left his mouth. His head rocked back while his neck spurted larger amounts blood. He grunted in pain and fell forward just missing Heron. The sword in his neck stabbed even further as the handle met the ground. He laid lifeless and defeated on the blood soaked battlefield and Heron stood still, shivering in fear and slowly shifting his eyes to confirm that Bazetar was out.

In the distance Kragnus continued fighting with his black double swords. They were as one until he removed the joining mechanism and revealed two razor sharp blades given to him by Bazetar. He expertly hacked at the mortals until something caught his eye. He saw his lord face down on the grass and the little prince standing over him. As the rest of his kin started to see this, their resolve began to wane till it was gone. In an instant, thousands of Trowcans began to flee the battlefield. Kragnus, still staring at Bazetar on the ground lightly growled.

"Well I see that even the most powerful can be complete fools. Oh, my great king. You have failed all of us." He turned to his remaining troops and gave the signal for a full retreat.

"All is lost my kin! We must flee. Every Trowcan for themselves!" The once great gray mass was now a shadow of its former self. The vast majority were slain, laying on the ground. Many of the Kreshant troops tried to follow the Trowcans now in full retreat but were quickly ordered to maintain the line by their captains. Though they were defeated, they could still regroup and attack again. A great roar could be heard from all the mortals who cheered their victory against inconceivable odds. They forgot the dead and injured for a moment and thanked the gods for this victory. Those left standing would all be going home to their families.

Not all were cheering though. There were a many great warriors littered around the battlefield, and many bore the mark of consumption by hungry Trowcans. There were very few wounded on both sides because they were all extremely efficient killers. Heron was now crouched next to his father as Elsia gracefully floated down. She sat next to the dying king and supported his head with her bare folded legs.

"The sounds of battle fade. How did we do?" asked Crenon with labored breath.

"We did well my lord, the Trowcans flee. Bazetar lays defeated on the ground. For now." Elsia adjusted her thighs to fully and comfortably prop Crenon's head so he could have a quick look around.

"It won't be long now my great friend. Where is my son?"

"I am here father." Heron's voice broke up as he answered.

"Do your old father a favor, grab my crown. It flew off my head when I hit the ground." Crenon was barely able to lift his arm to point in the direction of his royal crown. Heron quickly moved to retrieve it.

"I'm so sorry Elsia. Your people did not deserve this." Crenon coughed up blood.

"My good friend, rest and know that we are at peace having fulfilled our duty to you and your kind. We helped you overcome great adversity. It was our obligation to ensure your survival at any cost. Even if it meant the extinction of all the Enchantrics." She looked away from the dying king to hide her tearing eyes. The tears glistened as the sun began to poke through the retreating gloom that followed the Trowcans.

"Here it is my father. Here is your crown." Heron held it out, forgetting that his father had no more strength left in his battered body.

"Put it on your head my son."

"But, father, I ..."

"Do as your father says boy."

"Yes father." He held the crown over his head and slowly slid it on. There were gaps to the sides that his growing head still had to fill and it hid his eyebrows from view. Crenon smiled and let out one solitary tear from his left eye. He was never prouder of his son than at that moment.

"All hail the new Sagen King." He said weakly with his last bit of strength and then fell limp. His head hung loosely in Elsia's arms.

2

"Well that was a bit sad." Proclaimed the voice of a child.

"Why master Stosay? Why did the king and all but one Enchantric have to die?"

"Well my child, if we want a good story, then a few drops of blood must be spilt." Answered Stosay as he adjusted the white ever smiling mask he wore on his face.

"If we want a great story, then there must be red rivers." The children's eyes widened as they looked to each other in awe and fear. The children wondered how he was able to remain completely covered and why he never seemed to sweat though his garments were thick as they were.

"Master Stosay, what happened next?"

"Well my child," he turned the page,

"The evil god of the dead needed to be dealt with, but no magic was strong enough to kill him, so the next best thing was imprisonment. "

"So they put him in the brig?"

"Something like that my boy... Elsia, being the endless protector she was, made a prison for Bazetar using the last of her power. She too disappeared in puff of smoke leaving only a tiny piece of her wing. The piece of her wing became a treasured artifact of Heron's."

"Oh no." cried out a little girl, "She was my favorite."

"Bazetar's prison was a colossal rock golem that held a

small mountain over its head. There at the very top was a cell protected by a barrier made of Elsia's magic. Once he recovered his strength he tried to break free but it was useless. The barrier would rip off bits of his skin if he touched it. "

"Have any of you heard of the Flying Queen?" the entire class nodded no.

"Well, after the coronation of King Heron at the age of 12, his mother had dinner with him and said her goodbyes. She then walked up to the Eagle's Lookout and flung herself over the edge unable to bare the loss of Crenon. She fell from such a height that her body was obliterated leaving only a stain. The Orphan King Heron was truly alone. Thankfully there was still his uncle Matiun who helped him learn to be a fair and just ruler. Heron then became an adult, married his queen and sired three children. He was never able to shake the fear of Bazetar still being alive and close by. The events of the Rise of the Trowcans haunted his dreams and gave him frequent panic attacks. He was known to be nervous all his life."

"Now settle down so we can begin the next chapter." The children quieted down and listened to the story sayer.

Nwendor's Fate

He stood there in his chains with his head hanging low. All around him was the murmur of the divine jury. He felt so much anger, rage, and sorrow. How could he have let this happen to his beloved wife? Nwendor was a lesser god, son of the war god, Aires. He was always obedient and compliant with the laws of the gods for ages. Then one day a young, beautiful damsel caught his eye. She was a simple peasant girl who was on her way to the creek to fetch water for her household. Irlan was bent over, passing her jug under the water. In a quick motion she brought it to her chest and made her way back to the village. As she began to walk a figure blocked her way, startling her.

"Norques! You frightened me! What are you doing here?"

"I have simply come to admire the view." he eyed her up and down making Irlan extremely uncomfortable. She held the jug even tighter to her chest and broke eye contact with the man that was twice her age. Norques had long grey hair and slightly creased skin on his face. He was a bit portly and often wore an unbuckled tunic in an attempt to hide his overindulgences.

"My sweet lady Irlan, have you given my question any thought?" he smiled confidently at the young woman, again eyeing her slender frame indiscriminately.

Norques, I'm sorry but my answer is no. We are not a good match, and I do not harbor those feeling towards you. Please understand."

"My lady Irlan. Can't you see, I am here to become your lord? You'll never want for anything as my status will provide for us and our offspring. Your only duties will be to me. Come now; let the man decide what is right for you. It is the way of our people and the village."

"No, definitely not. I will not ever be your servant or slave, or any other notion you carry in that head of yours. Leave me be." She stormed off quickly without giving Norques another glance. Norques stood there in utter humiliation. How could this low born trash turn down his more than generous offer? To him, she was an ungrateful peasant that now needed to be taught a lesson. He gritted his teeth and contemplated his next move. Irlan continued walking towards her home. She constantly looked behind her to make sure Norques was not following. Once she was sure he was gone, her pace relaxed and she gave a sigh of relief. She continued on when suddenly an unknown voice asked her question.

"Why was that man trying to own you?"

"Who said that? I'm not afraid." she was visibly shaking and little droplets of water were falling on the collar of her dress from the clay jug. A dark figure of a man walked up to her, his eyes were glowing against the darkness of the forest shadows. As he drew closer, he left the darkness and was hit with sunlight.

"The man was clearly trying to purchase you, but curiously you were able to choose whether or not you'd be his." Irlan gazed at the man before her and was at first stunned by his looks and dress wear as they were not customary to her village. After the initial shock she regained her composure and sneered at him.

"Another man unable to control what comes out of his air hole. No manners were taught to you by you mother, clearly." Nwendor looked puzzled. He had merely asked a question, and this mortal had scorned him.

"I do not have a mother. I was made."

"Well then, whatever thing made you did a poor job."

"Do you know who you are talking to?" Irlan shrugged at him and walked away with her chin held high. She did not reply to him as she continued on her path back to the village. She kept walking and only turned back after she left the tree line. She was now in an open grassy field with stems reaching past her waist. Luckily, there was a small, barely visible trail. As she followed it she noticed that all the sound stopped. The birds stopped chirping, the insects stopped buzzing, and even the breeze stopped, amplifying the humidity in the air. Irlan stopped in her tracks and began to show growing concern for her safety. She looked in all directions and was afraid that maybe the man from the forest or even Norques might be out to get her. Her breathing intensified and her eyes moved frantically around trying to spot her would be attacker. Suddenly it happened. Her ears caught a buzzing sound approaching. At first she thought it a mere insect, but then saw what it was. It was a Zancoid. A human sized creature that had the features of an insect, with beating, buzzing wings, large compound eyes, arms like a mantis, and a long tail ending in a stinger. There had been reports of children from the village disappearing out in the outskirts and this must have been the culprit. Irlan let out a scream that came from the depths of her very soul. The water jug fell from her arms and shattered on the ground soaking it in all her labored effort. She took flight trying to reach a possible hiding spot in the forest. The creature was gaining on her with its mantis like arms raised ready to snatch her of the ground. The Zancoid had a venomous bite that liquefied its prey into a soup it could drink up. She looked back at the monster and saw that outrunning it was impossible. She stopped, gasping for air, and looked down at the ground for a possible weapon. Irlan found a fallen branch that could be swung as a club. She bent over to grab it and held it over her shoulder in a batter's stance. It seemed like hours went by as the Zancoid closed the distance between them. The creature's wings kept beating in a quick succession to where it could hover. A clear liquid oozed from its mouth and its arms were in attack position. After a long hiss, the creature shuddered and Irlan screamed too scared to swing her branch. At the moment the attack commenced the Zancoid moved violently to the right. It was wrapped in the arms of the lesser god, Nwendor, who had tackled it with such force and speed that they flew through the air. They impacted the ground and the Zancoid wiggled and writhed as Nwendor picked it up with one arm. The Zancoid's greenish brown blood spurted into the air. His right arm was held at his side ready to strike. Irlan followed his forearm down to his wrist, then hand, and to her surprise he had blades coming out of his fingers. The blades were long and slender reaching down to his ankles. Nwendor extended his arm and took a swipe at the creature. The long body fell to the ground and collapsed into separate pieces. The monster twitched as Nwendor lowered his left arm and dropped its lifeless head. He looked at Irlan with droplets of Zancoid blood peppering his face and flowing down his arm. All she saw was her savior, and ran over and embraced him. She began to cry as the fright was too much for her. He looked down at her with a crinkle on his brow. Why was this mortal holding on to him? He felt he should pull away but was rather smitten by her. Her touch was soft, and her smell was that of flowers. She loosened her arms and looked up at Nwendor. Their eyes fixed on each other as her tears started lighten. In a quick motion she wiped the excess from her eyes and reached up to grab the back of Nwendor's neck.

"Thank you."

He wanted to pull away but, her look, feel and smell were

entrancing. He could not resist her as she softly and moistly planted a light kiss on his lips.

A long time passed and Nwendor and Irlan developed a deep unconditional love for each other. He always arrived to meet her in secret as the gods were not allowed to interfere with humans directly. Attel forbade it after the debacle with Bazetar. Irlan would sneak away from her parent's home at different times so as to not arouse suspicion among the village folk. Aside from her parents no one would notice her missing except for Norques. He was growing evermore suspicious and noticed that she was completely avoiding him when before he would run into her often. That was his tactic, to slowly wither down her defenses, her will, and then he would have her all to himself. All the women and girls he had done this to were either discarded or disappeared without a trace. As time progressed, he began to pester Irlan's parents for her whereabouts but they never had an answer for him.

One-time Norques finally ran into Irlan as she walked through the village with a basket full of cloth for knitting.

"My lady, your presence has been missed. Are you well?" Irlan cringed and rolled her eyes as she knew the voice behind her well. She spun around and there he stood with his conniving smile and despicable eyes used to invade every inch of her.

"My lord, I did not see you. I..."

"Well, this is why you need me around. Imagine having servants do this drudgery for you. Ha! It's all they're good for. All you would have to do is cling to my arm." IIe snapped his fingers in the air and a maiden ran out to him with her head facing downwards.

"Grab her basket and take it to where she is going." the servant girl reached for the cylindrical basket and tried to take it but,

Irlan quickly pulled away. The girl turned to her master and gestured that there was nothing she could do. Norques raised his hand and struck the girl making her grunt in pain.

"Sorry wench! I'll do it myself!" He then reached for the basket and tried to pull it from Irlan. She fought back and tried to keep hold of it but Norques, though not being a particularly strong man, wrenched it free from her grip and exposed her raised belly. Norques and his servant girl looked at Irlan in complete astonishment. Irlan looked at them in horror. Her secret was out and the consequences would be dire.

"You are with a child?" yelled Norques while throwing down the basket with pieces of cloth to make baby clothes.

"Look, all of you, at this woman! She walks among you, trying to hide her despicable sin. She has the child of some miscreant. She has his bastard!" The crowd around them began to swell with curious onlookers. Irlan was scared but overcame it when she heard Norques' comment toward her baby. She became enraged, balled her fists, and stood defiantly against her attacker.

"You horrible beast of a man. How dare you insult one who is nothing but innocent and pure? The gods have a place for you, and all men unable to secure for them a conquest, without resorting to evil and cruel tactics. You sir are the lowest of the low while the child I carry will be greater and more powerful than anything you could dream of in that adolescent head of yours." A couple of arms reached out and pulled at Irlan, urging her to follow. They belonged to her father with her mother following closely behind. They quickly directed her through the crowd, into alleys and down the steps into their humble basement apartment.

Nwendor was told of the event, and was hell bent on revenge, but was talked down by his love and now secret wife. The ceremony was held at midnight under a full moon. Both of Irlan's parents were present and though they were afraid of what could happen, they loved their girl and always supported her unconditionally.

A few months later Irlan gave birth to baby girl. They named her Nyka and she was the light of their eyes. The pregnancy and birth were particularly difficult for Irlan as the child possessed godly strength inherited from her father and amplified her movements in the womb. Still all was fine and both mother and daughter were in good health. Irlan loved Nyka to the point she could barely put her down.

One day, Nwendor went to meet his father Aires as he had duties of war to tend to. Aires stood on a ridge overlooking a battle about to take place. The two sides were lined up about 100ft from each other. Taunts and other vulgarities were being flung around as the officers contemplated the best time to strike. The reason they were fighting was petty and unreasonable as both nations had a reputation for being.

"Hello father." Nwendor slid down the side of the ridge to reach his Aires.

"My son, the battle commences. As soon as the words left Aires the two sides ran at each other and began their duel.

"I favor the Ackshale tribe as they honor me in all they do. So, I gave the Arits a small outbreak of the stomach malady. Now, not all of them have it and they are more formidable so it should be a semi-fair fight." Nwendor looked in the direction of the battlefield, and yet his gaze was home with Irlan and Nyka. He knew what he was doing was expressly forbidden but he could not help his emotions.

"Did you listen to a word I said?"

"Oh, yes of course. The soldiers are good at running."

"Just as I thought you were not listening. What is on your mind?" asked Aires.

"Nothing, all I know is this battle and only want to......" Aires crossed his massive arms with the bladed one resting on his left arm. He gave his son an incredulous look and tilted his helmeted head slightly.

"Okay father I am lying." Nwendor was a brave warrior, always up for battle, but he was not up to taking on his father. Aires was easily five times his size and rivaled Bazetar in strength.

"I am done being a god. I want to live among the mortals. This was never the place for me."

"The mortals? Do you know what you are requesting? The loss of everlasting life. You will die eventually, and who knows if life's trials will send you with us or the plains of sorrow. Think before you go about making this decision."

"I have father, and I have for a long time. I will renounce my godhood tomorrow before Attel and I will live the humble life of a mortal, and who knows, even become a family man." Aires, though a war god was very pleasant. He derived his power from battles and worship from the most violent of the world but, was himself, kind and courteous. The thought of having a grandchild slightly thrilled him but he would never show it, always maintaining his composure around all who gazed upon him.

"Son, I knew this day might come, as we are gods, and the chance of you replacing me or another elder are slim. I know you long for something of your own and you know where to find it." Aires paused and stared at the carnage down below. Blood and entrails carpeted the ground. Hacked limbs and wriggling recently dead twitched under the feet of thousands still engaged in battle.

"Fine then my son. Go to where you believe your path is. I will always be there to guide you and hopefully we can meet again soon." The two engaged in a warm hug even as many descended to the plains of sorrow below them.

"Go now! Enjoy the world of the living. I hear the emotions are far more keen than that of us immortals."

"Farewell Father!" Nwendor ran off in speed far greater than that of a mortal and leapt many feet and distances without hurting a limb or even breaking a sweat. He had a great distance to cover to return to his beloved to give her the good news.

As night fell Irlan knitted a one pieced suit for Nyka who gurgled and babbled in her crib. The fireplace was crackling and Irlan eagerly awaited her husband's arrival. She hummed a soothing lullaby as Nyka drifted off to sleep.

Suddenly she got the feeling that something was wrong. Something dark approached her home and just as she stood to retrieve Nyka, the front door flew open knocking her down and making her hit her face on the floor. As she tried to get to her feet hooded figures barged in and grabbed her arms. She struggled and called out to her Nyka who was now wailing in her crib. One of the intruders heard the infant and kicked the crib over making the baby fall out violently. Irlan bit the arm of one of the men who yelled in pain. Another man brought his fist into her stomach, which make her buckle and gasp for air. As quickly as they had entered the little home, they left, and dragged the mother out into the night.

As her breath came back she regained her mobility. She raised her head and saw that the entire village was gathered at the main plaza. She had seen this before as the condemned were led here for their executions. The crowd sneered and called out obscenities as the woman was led through by the hooded men. Rocks, pieces of wood, and items of food were thrown at her as well as the men pulling her. There in the center was the terrible orchestrator of this attack. Norques stood with a torch in his hand next to an iron chair in the middle of the plaza. The chair was fastened to the stone bricks below that made up the entire plaza and there were many logs placed around it. Irlan could not believe her predicament. She was in utter shock as the hooded men forced her to sit in the chair and strapped her in. The smell of oil filled the air. She remembered all the executions she had attended before and how the victims screamed in agony. Also the smell of their searing flesh was unbearable. The villagers were always forced to gather and watch. Some enjoyed the spectacle while many others were revolted by the sights. Now here she was, just another name to add to the roster of those burned alive. She looked around in the breaks between the projectiles being flung at her and she saw her parents. They were holding each other and sobbing in anguish. They were powerless to stop the village authorities from carrying out Irlan's sentence.

"Order! Order! List now!" the crowd slowly began to quiet and all eyes fixed on Norques and Irlan.

"We are all gathered here in the night to push another sentenced sinner into the jaws of the Plains of Sorrow. She is a vile temptress, and a woman with the morals of a rabid dog." The crowd exclaimed in agreement.

"If anyone, myself included, decide to break our holy laws then they must be punished. Such actions have no place here as they corrupt our young as well as the adult." the crowd now louder scorned Irlan. She was still fixated on her parents as they were on her. She continued sobbing and could not even attempt to put words together, much less vocalize them.

"I have the permission and complete support of our honorable Judge Carns. He was so appalled by this woman's actions that he stated that no trial was needed for this crime of indecency." Norques pitched a look over to Carns showing that they were on the same page in this matter. Carns had been judge for years and was used to sending people to their deaths. He had been approached by Norques about the problem he was having with Irlan. At first Carns resisted the plea as a case of mere jealousy and told him it would be better for everyone to move on. He knew Norques was notorious for replacing women who had angered him in some way. The list of missing, executed, or plain dumped was a long one. Still, Norques held a very high status in the village. His family was wealthy and long held the positions of power. He gave Carns an ultimatum, that the girl be burned or he would not sit as judge, or be alive much longer. Carns relented and organized the execution of this woman whose only crime was that of love for her family. Though the laws were clear when it came to having children out of wed lock, it was never really enforced until now. Those who were usually sent to death committed more heinous acts. Still the villagers were convinced and trusted in the authority of the village leadership and earnestly believed that Irlan deserved her fate.

"Now with you permission my lord, I will send this horrid sinner to the Plains of Sorrow." Carns stared blankly into space. He did not want her to die and was slowly contemplating ways around her sentence.

"My Lord!" yelled Norques with sheer contempt on his face. Carns let out a pitiful sigh and with watering eyes gave the command.

"Let the torch fall." the crowd roared and Norques tossed his torch into the pile of logs and branches that were stacked under Irlan's seat. The fire quickly engulfed her hair and dress as the flames lashed at her skin. She wailed in agony so loud that the crowd's cheers began to die down. The villagers hushed up to where only the flames and the screams could be heard. Irlan's mother had fainted and collapsed on the ground. Her father sat next to her holding his head in his arms in disbelief. Her voice became hoarse from all her screaming and then she passed out from smoke inhalation and the pain. She never opened her eyes again. There she sat, the burned husk of what was once a loving, caring mother, wife, and daughter.

Later the flames died down and the crowd slowly began to disperse. Norques and Judge Carns viewed the smoldering remains still attached to the iron chair.

"You did well Carns, I expected no less from you."

"Shut your mouth Norques. This poor soul did not have to perish. If only you had the ability to control your ego."

"How dare you speak to me like that? I could have you hanged if I so please it."

"Do what you will. I am too old for these adolescent games you play." Carns had his hands behind his back and began to walk to his home a short distance away. He hoped the smell would not pollute the inside of his house.

"WHAT HAVE YOU DONE!" Nwendor's voice pierced the cool night air. Already his blades were unsheathed from the slit openings on the middle segment of his fingers excluding his thumbs. He walked over to the plaza with blinding rage seeping from his eyes.

"Who are you? Stop right there. Seize him!" commanded Norques. A band of 5 guards walked over to Nwendor with swords at the ready. In one swipe he removed the arm of the leading guard and his sword clanged on the ground. With his other clawed hand, he thrust into the man's chest leaving him lifeless. Another had his head removed instantly, while another was disemboweled. One of the remaining guards was knocked to the ground and had his head stomped to a bloody mass. The last guard tried to block the incoming bladed hand with his sword, but they cut through it and his face easily sending him to his death. Nwendor's attention then turned to all the villagers. None were spared. Swipe after bloody swipe, and stomp after bloody stomp all were murdered. Men, women, children and even pets and livestock weren't safe. When he reached his in laws he halted for a moment and stared at them. He was covered in blood and breathing rapidly. Irlan's parent tried to speak but he moved away quickly and continued his massacre leaving them be. After there was no more movement around him he began to walk towards the plaza where he knew Norques was hiding. He saw a conveniently placed pile of logs and approached it. Crouched behind it was Norques cowering in fear. One by one all the logs began to rise in the air, floating over Norques. There they stayed above his head surrounded by a faint blue hue of light. Suddenly they flew in all directions at great speed, crashing into the homes and other buildings of the dead villagers. Norques let out a whimper when he saw the blood covered Nwendor getting closer to him.

"Please! Who are you? Don't hurt me I beg you. I can make rich. Pleeeeeaaase!" he began to cry like a child while scooting backwards on the ground.

"I will show you the full extent of my mercy." A quick stomp and Norques right leg was shattered. Another and the other leg was broken. Norques was screaming in protest as if someone would magically come to his aid. He was so scared that the pain did not register. A downward punch aimed at his collar bone snapped it. Now the wounds were mounting and in a mortified labored gasp Norques felt the pain in all its sharpness.

"Please no more. Please stop."

"Now I will remove the thing that brought us all together this night. Your lying tongue!" and in fast actions Nwendor forced Norques' mouth open, grabbed on to and yanked it out from his mouth. The base of the tongue ripped free as blood gushed from the wound. Norques' eyes rolled into his head and there he bled to death with his mouth wide open.

Suddenly the sound of a twig snapping resonated in the silent village. Nwendor turned sharply and his eyes now with vertical slit pupils, fixed on the direction of the movement. It was Judge Carns. He had survived the slaughter by hiding under a mule cart and didn't make a sound even when Nwendor severed his wife's legs. From there he watched the life drain out of her as she blankly stared at him. He was trying to escape and Nwendor could not let that happen. He growled and ran at top speed towards the judge, drops of blood falling with every step. He leapt in the air raised a clawed hand and at the moment of ending the judge's life he dematerialized into thin air. Only a hazy golden mist remained and a few droplets even managed to sting Carns' face. Carns remained still, trembling in utter fright as his bladder and bowels relieved themselves all over his judge's gown. The only survivors of the massacre were Irlan's parents and the one who allowed it in the first place.

So there he stood for all to see, the lesser, the elder and all others who inhabited Attel's realm. All the gods resided here from those with important jobs to those whose tasks were to make the wine taste pleasant. Here is where he was sent after his rampage. He was to be judged by Attel, the lord of all the gods. Attel entered the room and all fell silent. All the divine beings showed him their unquestionable respect and the only one who had ever opposed him was Bazetar. He had the head of an elderly man with long white and ungroomed straight hair. His body was in the crossed legged seated position and wrapped in a heavy blanket with many geometric patterns. He sat on a flat circular surface with four long mechanical legs protruding from it. Each leg ended in a sharp point that stabbed the floor as it moved him around. In the center of the legs were many tendrils that could reach out and grasp, impale, or anything else he desired. This contraption was actually a group of thousands of solid objects held together and moving in unison with the power of his mind. Attel took his place on his pedestal and gave a nod to begin with the trial.

Knewt started the verbal assault on the defendant.

"Everyone welcome to the trial of our very own War Prince, Nwendor. Some of you will say he is brave, loyal, and even the spitting image of his father. He helps his Father get all the worship he needs to exist and is a good son." A few nodded their heads in agreement as other leaned in closer to listen.

"Of course, you would be wrong! He is nothing but a loathsome murderer!" Knewt pointed his long and thin finger attached to his long and thin arm. As he moved around the court hall with his tiny white wings flapping aimlessly as they were not big enough to lift him.

"He displayed cruel malice towards the mortals. He knew full well the power he had and yet he still sent them to the Plains of Sorrow in droves!" he paused for effect.

"An example must be made, he must be exterminated like that thing that bore his disgusting offspring." The spectators murmured amongst each other. Nwendor, again overcome with rage, extended his blades and made a motion to cut his shackles. It was impossible to do so as the chains were divine and impervious to anything but Attel himself. A giant sword rested gently on Nwendor's shoulder and he instantly calmed himself. It was his father, who was now making his way over to Knewt.

"Mind your tongue Knewt, you've made your point perfectly clear." The low deep rumbling voice echoed in Knewt's bowels and he shrank in demeanor.

"Yes my lord Aires."

"We await your decision my lord Attel. What is to become of Nwendor?" Attel walked as a spider would over to Aires and turned to address the other gods. He glanced at Nwendor and then back to the spectators.

"Never have I ever seen such anger, rage, and hate pouring out like a volcano for the mortals to witness. It was sheer luck that the girl's parents disappeared and the only witness left to this crime is considered a madman and was promptly committed." He turned his old wrinkled face to Nwendor and stared deep into his psyche and the very fabric of his existence.

"Son, Nwendor will be banished from here. He will live out his days amongst the mortals. The very ones he treated with extreme brutality. He will now be given a soul. It will be a record of his deeds and a constant reminder of his sins. It will weigh on him and pull him to the ground and eventually the Plains of Sorrow." The gods all murmured and then cheered Attel's sentence. Nwendor was led out of the court hall and outside to Helgon's bridge. Helgon was a mighty dragon that oversaw the placement of souls in the realm that corresponded with their actions in life. Nwendor stood at the center span of the illustrious bridge and did not meet Helgon's gaze. A grand snarl attracted his attention.

"Son Nwendor, you have been brought here to answer for your crimes. I am tasked with giving you a soul." Now that Nwendor's eyes were lock with Helgon's they could not be averted. He winced in emotional agony as he felt the deaths of all the mortals he had a part in. It was unbearable seeing the remains of his beloved crumbling before his eyes. He remembered Nyka, his baby was still down there and he had no idea where. He let out a blood curdling cry and collapsed to his knees crying uncontrollably. Helgon stopped and look over to Aires who signaled that it was time.

"Son Nwendor, your divinity is now gone. You will suffer as the mortals do. You will be allowed your godly powers as you may serve them and earn your place here or there." He pointed with his claw in the direction of the Plains of Sorrow.

"The choice is yours!" and with that the supports for the bridge were released. Only clean and righteous souls stayed, and all the others heavy with their burdens made the sections of the bridge swing open allowing them to fall through. The weight sent them crashing into the Plains of Sorrow where they would stew and wither in anguish for all time. Nwendor continued to wail in pain and was oblivious to the bridge that opened beneath him. The gods watched as one of their own descended past many layers of thick clouds till he disappeared.

Nwendor kept falling and as he did, he felt a sensation of heat all over his skin. The friction combined with momentum was making the heat grow ever more intense. Someone appeared next to him from thin air.

"Well, well, well, if it isn't the war prince himself." Though he was falling in excruciating torment, he was still able to view the one who spoke to him. It was Migus, son of the storm god Relo.

"Leave me, I should've know a fiend like you would show up to relish my fall." Migus let out a guttural laugh and his eyes began to glow as he easily held his upside down position in order to be face to face with Nwendor.

"More than you know. Here is a parting gift from me. I hope you enjoy it." And one of Migus' hands began to glow and rays of electricity flowed through him. He pointed at Nwendor and let loose a bolt of lightning that blasted the war prince and covered his already heated body in intense flame. Migus laughed and vanished back to the realm of Attel. Nwendor's plunge continued for what seemed to be an eternity, when it stopped abruptly when he hit the ocean. A giant vertical column of water reached for the sky as the fallen god disappeared beneath the waves. Nwendor felt the cool soothing sensation of water extinguishing the heat. His eardrums hurt and his lungs were desperate for air. He surfaced and took a giant gulp of oxygen which was something he never had to do before. Under the surface a dark shadow lingered and then leaped from the water. It was a Spiderbass the size of a house and had its toothed mouth agape ready for an easy meal. Before he could react the creature had snapped his jaws tight around the man and swallowed him in one gulp. As the fish's six eyes moved independently from one another looking for another meal, its mouth opened as a large blister formed on its underside. 4 blades pierced the fish's scales and its entrails poured out into the saltwater. It then floated to the surface and Nwendor climbed to the top and began to view the island before him. He contemplated making it his home or even ruling it with an iron fist. His mortal soul was staring to increase in weight.

On the shore there was someone who was watching from a distance. He had seen the unmistakable plume of smoke that could only be a banished divinity. He walked over to the location where the new soul would exit the water and waited. Nwendor waded ashore and was glad to feel the sand under his feet. He noticed something odd. The sand was composed of grains of gold. As he looked around for sign of inhabitants an apple sized ball of fire zipped by his head. He quickly got into battle position and faced in the direction from where it came. There stood Marcus, son of the fire god Yarma. Many years before Marcus had renounced his godhood because he fell for a woman as well. He went about it the right way and left Attel's realm before having any interactions with her. This was his territory and he was not going to allow this thug to take over.

"Nwendor, it is good to see you again. What brings you here to my island?"

"Your island? I was banished here and now seek a place of my own."

"You are on the land of the Yaga. They are indigenous here and do not like receiving visitors."

"Well, they will soon learn to bow to their new king."

"Perhaps we can come to some agreement to divide the island between ourselves. Or we can use brute force to settle our differences." Marcus was a giant of a man. He was almost 7ft tall and was built like a mountain. He was at least 300lbs of solid muscle and was an adept brawler. In his hand was the large grip of a massive sword almost as long as he was tall. It was the Sun Piercer, given to him by his father when he left. The blade was as wide as a man's torso as it rested on his shoulder.

"My family resides on the northern end of the island. We are all farmers and live a life of relative peace. You do what you will with the rest but I will have no encroachments on my territory. Do we have a deal?" Nwendor stayed quiet and stared at the man that towered over him. His claws slowly retracted back into the slits on his fingers.

"We have a deal my good sir, no encroachments of any

kind. I will see to it personally that my subjects do not scare your humble peasant farmers." Nwendor grinned at Marcus who was trying to decide whether or not he'd have taken the comment as an insult or brush it off. Before his decision was made Nwendor began to walk away towards the jungle with a smirk on his face.

"Farewell old friend!" he shouted behind him with his left hand raised. Marcus thought this arrangement was going to come back and haunt him in a way he did not fully understand yet. As he stood there he heard a roaring sound coming from the sky. He looked up and saw the tell-tale sign of a divine being falling from grace. Nwendor looked and followed the smoking fireball until it to crashed into the sea. He did not want to stay to find out who the individual was. He had more important things to do.

On a sunny afternoon by the perfect and beautiful waterfall called the stallion's tail was a group of Boe Chantrans enjoying the pool where the water collected. As long as they stayed away from the area where it drained to form a river they were safe. On this day there was a group of very voluptuous and scantily clad ladies. Their garb was white and they didn't seem to care how revealing they were. With them was a tall, slender, and well-built man who was bathing in all their attention. He performed stunts by flinging himself of the rocky ledges in numerous different ways to the glee and cheers of the women. He had a great love for himself and his sculpted looks. As he performed a particularly difficult leap with a combination of back flips, he lost his stride during the flips and a small jolt of electricity left his finger tip and struck a branch near the onlookers. The branch broke off the tree and fell harmlessly on the ground. Migus' eyes grew large as he read the looks of the stunned bathers. It was a disaster, he was found out and now he would surely face the same fate as Nwendor. Then the cheers flooded the air, the crowd loved it, especially the women he was trying to impress.

"Again! Again! Again!" was chanted by the crowd and with renewed enthusiasm he began shooting bolts of lightning and striking the cliff wall. As each bolt hit a boulder it was obliterated, and tiny particles rained down on the entertained watchers. Unbeknownst to everyone, the cliff acted as a wall that held back a massive reservoir. The Stallion's Tail merely drained the excess when it over flowed. Migus was jubilant. He had the praise of the crowd and had the full attention of the fair women, but suddenly he saw water beginning to burst through in highly pressurized streams. One of his admirers was hit in the gut by a stream and fell 30ft to her death. Migus tried to think of something her could do to save everyone, but it was too late. In one motion the entire wall of rock and dirt came apart releasing tons of water. The flash flood washed everyone away and headed to a nearby community causing a devastating flood. In mere minutes Migus had been the cause of thousands of deaths. He emerged from the flood waters many miles from his original location. The torrent had created a new lake as far as the eye could see. He stood on the roof of a collapsing structure as complete shock enveloped him. He began to glow and dematerialized into a cloud of gold particles.

3

"So it was like that, the three lesser gods ended up together on the unnamed island of the Yaga. They relieved the local royal family of their crowns and banished them to a group of three islands they named, "The Exiles." Only the most loyal of their court accompanied them there, and the rest stayed to be subjects of the new rulers. The island was divided in three section and was given the name Tridom. Walls were erected and the locals were divided into 3 factions where constant turmoil existed in everyday life. The three kings, including Marcus, erected their own palaces, forts, as well as a central arena where the three walls met at a point. There, all differences could be sorted out without a full on war. Tridom was also closed off to all trade and contact with the rest of the world as per the orders of the lesser gods."

"So how is it that Migus zapped Nwendor, and in a short time was already banished?" asked Amon.

"Well you see time does not exist in the realm of Attel. It does not follow our perceived notion of a steady, continuous flow. A man can die and his wife die 30 years later, but he will feel that only a blink of an eye has gone bye. That is how the lesser god Migus was able to attack Nwendor, go to commit his crime, and receive a trial, all in mere moments."

"What? What does all that even mean?" asked Crux.

"We are spending too much time on this topic. You young minds need to mature bit before you can grasp this notion. Let's move on, our next chapter is about the royal family of Kreshant."

The Sagens

The Sagen royal family gathered at the port of Sagen. They were there to bid farewell to the king, queen, and Prince Abel. They were about to embark on a diplomatic mission to Tridom. The goal was to open trade and communications with the rulers and maybe even form a protective pact. The twin sisters Sarre and Sadanasia would be left in charge of the country as well as caring for the royal heir, Xenon.

"Goodbye my precious daughters. We love you and will miss you." The now 60-year-old Heron hugged his girls. Sarre's eyes grew watery while in her father's embrace. Sadanasia stood with her arms crossed and was annoyed and indifferent as always. The twins were quite different, as Sarre was always viewed as the, "good one" and Sadanasia was always the, "bad one." Sarre held her hands close to her face as her father pulled away to wipe off her tears. Sadanasia simply pulled away with a frown on her face. She would have preferred to have stayed in the Castillo Morta tending to her own personal matters instead of this. She turned to look in the distance avoiding eye contact with her parents.

"You will be the least of my concerns my boy!" Heron grunted loudly as he lifted Xenon and held him high. The 8-year-old was very rambunctious and struggled to break free of the king's grasp while laughing loudly. He set the boy down and Sarre pulled him towards her, holding his shoulders against her waist. Xenon became calm in his sister's iron grip and focused on his parents.

"Remember Girls, protecting our home protects our legacy. I know I can trust you both"

"It is time to leave sire!" Matiun cried out from the ship's quarterdeck. The old man was going as strong as ever and eager to visit Tridom. He continued to fulfill his duties of advisor and defense coordinator for the kingdom.

"My girls, you are now the rulers of Kreshant until our return. May the gods guide you down the path of wisdom and glory." The captain ordered raised anchors and the ships began to traverse the harbor. The king and queen waved to the pier and went on to address the crew. Prince Abel stood at the ship's rails waving to his half sisters. He was the son of the queen from her previous marriage. He was only 4 when his father, King John of Brethen Paya was assassinated during a failed coup attempt. When the army of Kreshant arrived to assist, their lonely young king met his current queen. Over the extent of the occupation he and she grew close as he comforted the widow. They became intimate over time and he eventually proposed marriage. She renounced any claim she or her son had to the country and left to rule Kreshant. Brethen Paya was taken over by the late king's younger brother Tetso.

Back on the pier Sarre still waved as little Xenon began to chase the resting sea birds. Sadanasia had left as soon as the gangway was lifted not really caring if they ever came back. Sarre, on the other hand, was overcome with anxiety. She was coached on how to best run a kingdom, and the Kreshant one was the most powerful of them all. Surely there was no possible way she could destroy her own civilization in a few weeks. Though it was overwhelming, she was determined to serve her country well and help it continue to prosper. She would bet her life on it.

"Princess Sarre!" Sarre let out a yelp as she turned to address her court counselor.

"Sorry my lord. You surprised me."

"Your order your highness?" he held his chin up and

stared at the young delicate woman before him.

"Where is my sister?"

"She walked away with haste. I don't know where she went." Sarre lightly stomped her heeled foot on the ground in frustration with her sister.

"Okay then, launch the regular night patrols and gather the council in the meeting chamber." The counselor bowed and then walked away urgently. They were supposed to handle this together, she thought, and now it seemed like she would be doing all the work by herself. She walked down the pier with Xenon while escorted by her personal guard and rode on horse back to the castle.

Sadanasia had already arrived. She had ridden back in a carriage manned by her guards and made her way to her chambers. Though it was immaculate, the room was only so because of the hard work of the servants. In all her life she had never performed a single bit of labor or any other menial task. She walked about her room waiting for something to happen. She looked out the window impatiently. There she could see the mountain golem holding up Bazetar's mountain prison.

"My love, how do you fare in that terrible place? I am here waiting for your response." She listened carefully for any sound but the room was completely silent. She heard passing footprint and flung her chamber doors open.

"I demand silence!" she yelled at an apologetic old servant woman in her 50's.

"Make another noise and I will have you arrested. Do you hear me?" the woman bowed frantically and quickly left the vicinity. Her chamber was located in one of the numerous giant round towers that made up the Castillo Morta. The room was huge. It was far bigger and taller than any structure located in the city and with its towering window she was able to see all the happenings beneath her. Nothing interested her though. She was always bored, unhappy, and held contempt for everyone and everything.

That was how her life was until her 18th birthday. Her parents held a huge ball in her honor. It was packed with guests coming in from afar to wish the princess well. They would all be disappointed, as Sadanasia never attended finding much satisfaction in ruining the celebration. Heron was furious, and once she was found, gave her the biggest scolding he could ever muster. She ran to her room, slammed the enormous fancy door and wept on her bed. She declared her hatred for her parents, siblings, and all life in general.

Suddenly she heard a voice speaking in her head. The deep voice told her it understood how she felt and that she was special. It assured her that only it could set her free of her parent's tyranny. She asked the voice who it was. She felt fear at first but it was quickly melted away. It was Bazetar projecting himself from his prison into her mind. Slowly he caressed her self-importance, and narcissism. He made her feel intensely powerful and kept her in a constant state of euphoria to the point where she never wanted to leave her room. Her parents began to think she was possessed by an evil spirit. Sometimes her eyes became black abysses as she was shown unspeakable things from the Plains of Sorrow. He had convinced her that he needed to be freed from his prison in order to serve her better as his new queen. She was full of excitement at the idea of becoming a queen. She didn't even care about what would happen to the rest of her family as long as she got her due. Bazetar made a plan which she was to carry out now that her parents were away.

There in the king and queen's chamber was a small chest about the size of a brick, and it held something wonderful. It housed the sole piece of good magic left in the world. It was the tip of Elsia, the Enchantric's left wing. After she imprisoned the Troll King her body vaporized except for the remaining piece.

That sole item had more magic in it than any mages or wizards could ever conjured up. She was given the task of relieving her parents of it. She waited till nightfall when all the lights would be out to make her move. She slowly opened her door and walked out in her night gown, barefooted. She carefully closed her giant door that was surprisingly silent.

"May I ask where you're off to?" Sadanasia let out a shriek and turned to face her twin.

"Sarre, don't you ever sneak up on me like that." She clutched her heart while breathing heavily.

"You weren't at the meeting today. You left me to make all the decisions by myself. We are supposed to do this together. How will this make us look to our subjects?"

"You're right. I was not there and never will I be. Those meetings are all talk and work, and I have far more important things at hand."

"Like what? What could be more important than running a kingdom?" Sarre stepped a little closer to her twin's face.

"You seem to be handling it all just fine. I mean, the castle is still intact and the air is still breathable. What more could you ask for?" Sadanasia gestured as if she were dancing in a play and began to leave the chamber hallway.

"You are such an inconsiderate child! You're lucky to have a family that supports your arrogance and laziness!"

"My family won't be around much longer." Sadanasia said under her breath. Sarre grunted and stormed off followed by 2 guards. The lights outside the bedroom complex were all off and she could barely see anything. Sadanasia felt her way around the walls making for her parent's chamber.

"Do you need some assistance my beloved?" a low dark voice rumbled in her mind.

"Yes, I cannot see anything." She said aloud.

"Behold your king's power." Sadanasia felt a strange itchy sensation on her irises and began to rub them. When she was done, she had night vision. She clapped her hands and cried out in jubilation.

"Who's there?" cried out a castle guard. She fumbled with her starter stone trying to get a spark to light her torch. After a few strikes the sparks flew and the torch was burning. She held it out trying to see what made the noise, but Sadanasia was long gone. While the guard fumbled around with her equipment, the girl walked right by her in the shadows, and up to the royal chamber. Once inside the girl was greeted by a painting of the whole Sagen family. They all looked so noble and well kept. There were her nagging parents, her bothersome little brother, and her half-brother who always pushed her to better herself. She then looked at Sarre. They were supposed to be identical, but the years of frowning, and inactivity left her looking weaker and less attractive than her sister. She was always jealous of the looks the men around the castle gave her twin and not her. They always seemed to be avoiding her wherever she went. As her gaze shifted to her own likeness, and she was disgusted. There she was with her arms crossed and looking off to the side. She remembered how uncomfortable the dress was and could not wait to remove it and fling it from the window. Her parents now weary of her constant insolence and attitude commanded the artist to paint her in that unflattering pose. She let the voice guide her again.

"There it is. I can sense it through you." It told her that the massive painting was actually a swinging door and that the chest was embedded in a wall slot behind it. She undid a hidden latch and pulled the portrait so it could swing open. The wall behind the portrait was missing a few bricks in the center. She reached for the chest and pulled it free.

"Oh, what bitter tastes and smells are emanating from

that box. You must bring it to me." Sadanasia grinned felling she held his fate in her hands. Her conniving mind began thinking how long she was going to make him wait before she freed him.

"I will once the way is clear. We must not rush these things my lord." Bazetar grew silent trying not to provoke the princess. He sensed her mischievous thoughts and although he wanted to be free, he knew he needed Sadanasia. So, he played her little game and waited patiently in his cell. She hid the chest in her chamber under lock and key in her trunk at the foot of her bed and continued to play the bratty princess. Bazetar would still come in to her mind and keep her company, always whispering into her ear. All he needed was for her to have an emotional episode and go running to him for salvation.

The Sagen flotilla arrived at Tridom many days later. The three kings were each sent messengers and were curious to see why Kreshant was interested in them. They met the king and his entourage in the central arena which held 3 elevated thrones facing the centermost point of the island.

"My dear kings of Tridom! We come from Kreshant. The wealthiest and noblest of the countries of Boe Chantra. We would like to offer you a mutually beneficial agreement that would unite our great nations!" The Yagan citizens all murmured to each other as Matiun took a deep breath to continue his speech.

"Our great king and queen have made the long journey here to meet you personally. You are all that important to us. Please allow us to come to terms with you." Matiun backed away as his old voice still resonated in the arena walls. Heron walked forward wearing his royal attire with his hands behind his back. Marcus, Nwendor, and Migus sat in their thrones that surrounded Heron. Their elevated positions made it so the king had to look up to them where they sat. Marcus was sitting calmly with his sword resting on his laps, Nwendor looked at the Sagen king with his ever-present glare, and Migus was completely relaxed with one leg upon an arm rest and a drumstick in his right hand.

"Greetings my lords. It is good to finally meet you."

"Is it really Sagen?" Migus asked while chewing pieces of meat in his mouth.

"How is it that the King and Queen of Kreshant personally came all this way, not knowing if we'd even agree to their proposal or if they'd even be allowed to return home." He let out a chuckle and threw the bare bone into the air behind him.

"My lord, we are simply here as a sign of our friendliness towards Tridom and to assist in any way possible."

"Who said we'd ever need your help?" asked Nwendor leaning forward resting one arm on his knee.

"This is Tridom Sagen king. We have made this land what we wish of it. All the mortals bow to us and worship us and that is the way we like it. You and the rest of Boe Chantra are lucky we have not decided to branch out and bring the rest of you under our heel." Migus chuckled again while grabbing some grapes from a servant.

"You three are our link to the gods. You are from the realm of Attel and we wish to appease you and worship accordingly. We do it for our citizens as well as your own. Your subjects would benefit greatly from the increased wealth and security trade with us would provide."

"Our subjects will like whatever we say they will like. We are their masters and their sole reason for existing is to serve us." Said Migus.

"You have spoken for us long enough Migus." Interrupted Marcus.

"King of Kreshant, what you propose to us sounds promising. Long have we tried to keep this land out of the affairs of the surrounding kingdoms, but I feel we are doing our subjects a great disservice. Our people can trade goods, services, and ideas. It is something I have long been considering, and you arriving at our doorstep just makes my decision that much easier. If my compatriots choose not to join, then it is their own choice. Tridom Marcus is with you."

"Splendid my King Marcus." Heron bowed his head.

"Oh, come on Marcus. Will you just fold that easily when flashed a little coin? Luckily Nwendor and myself are not swayed in any direction with such ease." said Migus.

"Great King Heron. Like Marcus said we have been isolated for a very long time. My daughter Nyka knows nothing of the outside world. I fear it is having a detrimental effect on her. Who is to say she will not embark on her own one day because the pursuit of foreign interaction was forbidden. No, I think I will not let it come to that. You can count on Tridom Nwendor."

"Wow my fellow gods. You have really just let these mortals come in and try to treat with us. Unacceptable! Why don't we just let them move in to our palaces where they can eat our food and court our.... Wait a minute. I don't suppose you brought some ladies over here have you?" asked Migus.

"We travel with a huge fleet of warships manned by 10,000 soldiers, 5,000 sailors, hundreds of servants, and an assortment of ladies in waiting my lord." Heron smiled as Migus stroked his chin and contemplated.

"Okay lord Heron, I will grace you with the gift of my partnership. Rejoice!" Heron's entourage cheered as did the Yaga.

Later that evening a celebration was held at the central arena. Music and the smell of food filled the air. There was laughter and joy around every turn. Heron sat at a huge table with many different things to eat. Queen Leta was at his side taking in the different look and culture of the Yaga. They wore long feathers in their hair, walked without shoes, and wore significantly less cloth than they did. They had to be way more comfortable than she was with her binding evening gown, and heavy jewels.

"I will be back in a moment my dear." Heron excused himself and walked away from the festivities to relieve himself. A detail of guards, along with Matiun waited outside for him. The door to the privy opened and out he came adjusting his belt.

"Hello Sagen king." The guards snapped to the ready and the king flinched at the voice coming from the tree. It was Nwendor relaxing on a high branch enjoying a bottle of ale.

"Lord Nwendor. You startled us." Nwendor hung his feet from a side of the branch and fell feet first to the ground 16ft below. There was almost no sound when he landed like that of a cat. He took a drink from his bottle and stared at the king's guard still holding their weapons.

"Men please sheathe your swords and leave us." The guards reluctantly backed away and sheathed their swords.

"You men heard your king. Let's go before I get a heart attack from any more of these surprises." Matiun led the men away.

"Your guards are very loyal; I'll give them that." The glow faded from his eyes as he slowly began to walk next to Heron. They followed a path that led to a high ridge overlooking the harbor. Flying insects lit the night air and a cool breeze flowed through the land.

"Such a beautiful island you have here. It has not yet been corrupted by the Bole Vans and their greedy practices or raids by the Surrians. There is just pure tranquility. A rare place to find in these times."

"The Yaga would've removed any foreigner's head and would have paraded them in the streets before we came. The

Wrell family are the original rulers and were pretty good at governing before we came, but engaged in odd practices. It is tranquil now that we are here."

"I am glad. Who knows what indecent rituals the Yaga would've started had you not set them straight." Nwendor looked down at the ground and thought of all the families that were separated when the island was divided. It was a terrible ordeal suffered by almost all the Yaga. He raised his gaze to get his mind off the thought and was amazed at the sight of the numerous warships in Tridom Harbor.

"You brought quite the royal guard to this meeting. It seems like you were going to try to get your way by any means necessary." Nwendor stared coldly at Heron waiting to hear the King's response. Heron began to stammer trying to find the right words to assure Nwendor they were no threat.

"Great King Nwendor, we merely travel with the utmost caution. We have many enemies and there are those who would undo us at the slightest show of weakness."

"Good King, I personally knew you came here with no ill will. I could sense it the moment you approached our throne room and addressed us all. I was ready to accept your terms even before began talking to us. As you know my daughter Nyka is young and full of curiosity. I can't keep her here for much longer. Perhaps you can take us on a personal tour of Kreshant one day."

"It would be my pleasure friend." Heron extended his heavily ringed hand and Nwendor took it accepting their new partnership.

At the celebration, a young woman with long white hair and tanned skin walked out into the crowd. She saw the Yaga dancing their traditional dances which she knew quite well. She did not partake as she was on a mission to find a Sagen. She walked past the food table littered with all kinds of different entrees from fish to red meat. She continued looking around the festival when her eyes caught the sight of a man sitting with a detail of knights. He sat on a table with one leg on the chair and the other on the floor. He was sipping a goblet with a type of wine made by the Yaga. As he drank his peripheral vision caught the gaze of the woman locked on him. He paused from drinking and smiled at her with the cup still up to his lips. She saw the smile and did not react. Her stare remained constant and her expression one of sternness. Abel put his goblet on the table and lifted his armored body from the table. He excused himself from his detail and walked casually over to Nyka.

"Good evening, madam. How are you tonight?" Able stood a good foot and a half over Nyka's height.

"What is your name traveler?" she demanded.

"I am Prince Abel of the country of Kreshant." he said with total confidence and a smile.

"Who might you be?" Nyka stood silent, studying the man before her. He kept smiling a conceitedly, waiting for her to say something.

"I want to know everything about your country and Boe Chantra." She tugged his hand and pulled him towards some chairs where they could talk. Abel cleared his throat and began a long lesson about his home country. History, geography, and various other topics involving the island continent it was a part of. Nyka's eyes were bright and lit up. Her hands supported her head as she leaned in closer. Not a detail would be missed. The conversation shifted over to her and her upbringing. They carried on through the night till most of the party goers had already left. Her cold demeanor melted away as did Abel's smug attitude. He no longer saw her as a no nothing, sheltered princess, but an interesting and intelligent young woman.

"Well, where has the time gone? It is so late." Nyka slapped both her thighs and stood. She did not wear a dress as Abel's sisters did. She was dressed in form fitting pants with knee-high boots. She carried a whip at her side and had many throwing blades tucked into slots that were woven into her pant legs. Nyka also wore shoulder armor and had a long thin sword hanging from her belt. Abel stood quickly and held Nyka's hand.

"My princess, will I see you again?" Nyka felt strangely attracted to the man and did not pull her hand away. She sighed and tried to speak.

"Nyka my love, there you are." it was Altor, her long-time suitor.

"I've been looking for you and wondering where you've been." He walked up and hugged her practically pushing Abel out of the way. He was dressed in the fanciest of clothes, different from Yagan traditional wear.

"Oh my good sir, thank you for guarding her majesty, but your services will no longer be needed. Good night to you." he held Nyka's arm with both hands as she giggled when she saw Abel's perplexed face. He gestured, "what just happened?" to her.

"Altor, this is the Prince of Kreshant, Abel." she smiled at him.

"Oh, I see. Well sir you have pretty boats but I must escort the princess to the palace. Let's go dear."

"They're warships." Said Abel defending his ships.

Nyka easily slipped out of Altor's grasp and walked over to Abel. She stood on her toes and gave him a soft and tender hug.

"Thank you." she whispered as he felt her warm breath caress his ear. She quickly moved away and took Altor's arm who was glaring back at Abel. Abel raised his hands with his palms out facing Altor. They walked away and Nyka turned one more time to give Abel a quick glance. He felt urged to go and court her but could do nothing but stay where he was.

"Nyka huh? We will be together always. Just you wait." A

splash of water slapped his face as two Yagan children laughed and ran away. He wiped his face of the water cursing the kids. He turned his head to the right and was greeted by the rising sun.

After a few days the Sagens packed up and prepared to depart for home. Abel snuck off many times to go see Nyka, who had to constantly remind him that she was spoken for even though she much more preferred his company than that of Altor. She really was sad to see him go. She turned to look at Altor who was off with his companions, a group of rowdy, ill-mannered ruffians. He was such a chore. She knew he was only around her for the status their union would bring him one day. She rolled her eyes as Altor chuckled with his friends about something she knew was definitely not funny. There went Abel carrying a bag of his belongings over his shoulder while boarding his ship. The rest of the Sagens boarded and soon the harbor was empty once again. All the citizens felt sad to see the fleet leave. It had been such a good time for all of Tridom. It was no coincidence that the following day, the leaders of Tridom sent out a royal decree stating that there would be free movement on the island. Families were reunited who hadn't seen each other for years. The light of Tridom was showing brighter than ever with a new found freedom and purpose.

The Sagens returned to Kreshant and the Kingdom rejoiced. They all returned to their appointed positions. Sarre was praised by her parents for running the kingdom as smoothly as she did. Heron was proud telling her he could not have done a better job himself. Xenon on the other hands quickly let everyone know that his governing would've been a million times better.

"Where is your sister?" his glee turned to displeasure. He knew the answer even before Sarre said that she was in her chamber and did not want to come down. Heron gritted his teeth and stormed up to her chamber. All along his ascent, Queen Leta asked that he keep his composure and think before he spoke to her, but it fell on deaf ears. He was out to get her this time. The doors to Sadanasia's room flew open and she was startled out of her bed. She was still wearing her nightgown.

"What are you doing up here Sadanasia! You did not make time to go greet us?"

"I was tired and just woke up." she lied. She had been awake for hours but wanted to upset her parents. She stretched, got out of her bed, walked over, and tried to give her father the most pitiful hug ever given. Heron pushed her away to where she almost stumbled and real tears began to fill her eyes.

"Your sister did all the work you should've done, for you! All you did was lounge about and go to gods know where! This was your one chance to redeem yourself and you completely failed!"

"Father I....." for once in her life she was at a loss for words. She was always one to make a sarcastic comeback then walk away. This time, however, there was something different in Heron's voice. His voice had a hint of defeat in it. She could feel her father giving up on her completely. She merely took the scolding while crying.

"I am tired of your slovenly ways my daughter. No responsibility, no usefulness, you are a waste of a person. We have tried remedy your total lack of motivation but failed you miserably."

"Father, stop please let me try to..."

"I am not finished!" he yelled directly into her face.

"You will go to the school of the gods and become a monk there. We will not have you here not pulling your weight or serving our people. We will enable you no longer."

"No! I will not go there! You can't make me!"

"Oh, but we can. You see I had a suspicion this is what we would come home to and made all the necessary arrangements before we departed."

"You. How dare both of you treat me this way!" angered by her father's decision she stopped crying and became enraged.

"You will not sit on the throne for much longer. I will be queen of this land for many years to come. Your time is up, I hate both of you!" her face jerked sharply to the left as the hand of her father slapped her. She turned back slowly with a look of shock all over her face. The tears had stopped flowing. She held her cheek and ran away without saying anything. Her mother called out to her but she didn't stop. Heron felt horrible for what he did. He didn't remember his father ever striking him at all, then again he would have never yelled at him either. It was the way she was shouting at them that made him lose his cool.

After a while, the king and queen left the princess' chamber and attended their royal duties. Sadanasia crept back into her room and took the Enchantric's wing piece with her. She dressed for a long journey and took a royal steed. She was not a particularly good horse rider because she never listened during training. Still, she was determined to get back at her parents. Most of the trip was up hill putting heavy strain on the horse. While ascending a rocky trail she kept whipping the animal until it bucked her off. She hit the ground and a pointed rock opened her elbow. She wept and screamed in pain. The small chest fell a few feet from her and the horse ran off. She managed to get to her feet and grab the chest with her good arm. It began to rain while night was setting in. Her hood protected her vision somewhat as she continued up the trail. The steady voice of Bazetar beckoned her forward relieving some of the pain from the gash in her arm. The rain eased, and then she realized she was at the foot of the massive Mountain Golem. The giant rocks in front of her were its toes. She saw the way up. It would be impossible to climb that with her injured arm. Bazetar reassured her that she could do it and that he would continue to help her. He arm was still bleeding but was no longer hurting. Now it was like having a mere bruise on your elbow.

The climb was a series of rungs and the occasional step. She felt no pain from her arm or fatigue as she reached an incredible height. The chest was in a satchel dangling from her back. Suddenly she lost her grip and began to slip. She let out a scream as Bazetar's invisible hand took over hers securing her back into place. After climbing for what felt like hours, she was at the prison entrance. There stood a lonely soldier shaking in his armor. He was almost done with his watch. Many soldiers had to be let go as the Troll King would infect their minds with corrupt thoughts. Many went mad while others committed horrible acts of violence against their loved ones. The new rotation called for a replacement after 2 days to allow the soldier time to get spiritual healing to overcome the effects. As the soldier shook not knowing if what he was seeing was real or a trick by Bazetar he lifted his pike to the ready.

"Who goes there!" the shadowy figure walked over to him and he lifted his torch to light up the area in front of him. He saw a woman-like creature snarl at him with vicious fangs. He screamed dropping his pike and ran out of the cave entrance. As he plummeted, he still moved his legs in a running motion while screaming; trying to escape the monster he had hallucinated. Sadanasia grinned at the cowardly man's fate and began to walk slowly to Bazetar's cell. She had expected bars but only saw a flat, black circular structure. She attempted to touch it but was zapped by a stinging light. She put her finger in her mouth to calm the burning sensation and called out.

"My love, I am here." no answer. She thought she caught a faint movement inside the black void. The inside of the cave began to light up dimly until she was able to see him. There was Bazetar walking over to her in all his might and malice. The former god of the dead stood on the other side of the barrier which turned out to be a clear see-through wall of magic. His eyes were glowing as he stuck his claw right through the barrier while grimacing in pain. Sadanasia yelped in surprise as the claw was much bigger than she had imagined.

"Give me the wing tip." Bazetar's hand was losing skin and the muscle and tendons were beginning to show.

"Yes my love, but first you must promise that I will be your queen." Bazetar winced in agony and agreed. Sadanasia clapped her hands, reached into the satchel and placed the chest in his claw. He closed his claw crushing the luxurious chest and revealing the magic wingtip. Instantly the barrier made an exclusion zone around him allowing him to simply stroll right out. He stood looking around the cave, feeling the cool breeze from the rainstorm outside. His glowing eyes fixed on the woman before him.

"So, you must be the woman that helped me escape. I am eternally grateful. He grabbed her from under her arms like one would a child and brought their faces together in a long kiss. Sadanasia was not at all repulsed by his look. There, that night he made her his queen.

Back at the Castillo Morta, the night was like any other night. The watchmen were at their posts and the servants were tending the halls preparing for the following day. King Heron and Queen Leta sat next to the fireplace in deep thought. Heron still felt horrible, he really wanted to take back what he had done. He even considered not sending her away to become a monk after all. He had been too rash in his thinking. He and his wife discussed their options but they always came back to sending her away. They knew she would never change and it was just the guilt that was making them consider enabling her again. The doorway to their bedroom flew open putting out the fireplace. The royals gasped at Sadanasia as she was in a long black dress. There was something different about her.

"Mother, Father, I have thought of what you told me and I agree with you completely. I should be sent away. It was my own selfish actions that got me here and I need to better myself." Heron and the queen were flabbergasted. Was it possible that simply striking their daughter worked this well? Heron ran over to her and hugged her tightly.

"My baby girl I am sorry." he let loose tears as did the queen who also joined the embrace. Sadanasia did not return the gesture.

"No need father. I was being overly obnoxious and to prove to you that there are no hard feelings, I have a gift for you in your study." the three walked hand in hand all the way to the study. The queen asked about Sadanasia's new dress. She told her smugly that she sewn it herself in her room. They stopped at the doors leading to the study and Sadanasia told them to wait.

"Close your eyes. It will be a grand surprise" she said with a smile. Her parents closed their eyes and felt relieved. They felt they had finally reached their daughter. The king decided in his mind that he would not send her off after all. He liked the new her and wanted to get to know her.

"Okay, open up!" the King and Queen slowly opened their eyes and received their grand surprise. There, right in front of them, stood the hulking Bazetar.

"Surprise you old fools!" laughed Sadanasia. The Troll King turned slowly to face them, eyes glowing and teeth bared. The queen screamed at the sight but Heron simply froze as a claw reached for him. He was transported to the time he was a child facing this same monster. Now here he was decades later in the same spot. Unlike his father Crenon, he could not grab his sword. Even if he was wearing it, he was simply too scared. Sadanasia's face lit up and she began to giggle with excitement.

"Heron." growled Bazetar's voice as the king suffered a massive heart attack the moment the Troll King's claw gripped his body.

4

"Wow. So that is what happened to King Heron?"

"Yes, the king and queen were slain and Bazetar took over as the new King with the treacherous Sadanasia by his side. It is said that the whole time her parents and countrymen were being slaughtered, her laughter echoed through the castle." Stosay adjusted his mask and continued the lesson.

"What did you mean by, "he made her his queen" back in the cave?" all the children began to laugh aloud as the boy was still perplexed. Stosay told the kids to settle down, and again they didn't hear him. He stood perfectly still as the holes for eyes in his mask stared off in the distance. A certain feeling of darkness filled the room and the kids grew scared. They looked at their teacher's mask and felt a low growl emitting from it.

"Now children as I was saying." he began instantly with the same energy and the darkness was gone.

"The kingdom was in ruin. Bazetar began to empty the Plains of Sorrow once again with his magic and the Trowcans were reborn. They poured forth from the Castillo Morta and decimated the armies of Kreshant and Boe Chantra. The gods sensed what was transpiring on Boe Chantra and tried to assist. They formed a shield sphere around the castle locking Bazetar in. The measure was temporary as they could not hold him there indefinitely. He would find a way out. Still his armies conquered country after country." Stosay's students were now quiet and listening and were too afraid to ask questions. He continued the lesson. He would much rather have these spoiled students quiet over everything else.

"Again the country of Bole Va was attacked. This time though they did possess a standing army and met the Trowcan horde. Sadly the Bole Van army was made up of rich citizens that went out in fancy bejeweled armor and began a practiced routine to scare off the Trowcans. They marched like a marching band with many complex movements and formations. Once the Trowcan army saw enough they charged and the high pitched screams could be heard for miles as the, "soldiers" were eaten alive. Those who resisted were made up of the Giants in the northeast, the Vampires of the northern mountains, the volcanic island of Diablo Surr, and of course Tridom." a nervous child raised his hand and Stosay turned sharply to face the child. The low growl was heard followed by a cheerful pleasant voice.

"Yes, my child."

"Master Stosay, what happened to Abel and Sarre during the takeover of the castle?" the child asked nervously.

"Good question, Sarre was taken prisoner by her twin sister and kept under constant watch by the Trowcans. Able escaped with his baby brother and most of the southern army. They sailed for the Gold Beach of Tridom.

"Boe Chantra was in shambles. The population of millions was reduced by a tenth of its original population. The death toll was overwhelming and still climbing. As the Trowcan armies advanced they would sustain heavy casualties but were replaced quickly by Bazetar's Magic. The column of Trowcans marching out of the Castillo Morta was constant. Kragnus had returned from hiding showing no sign of aging and was again placed in the command of the Trowcan northern army. He was tasked with the siege of Koglan, home of the giants."

"Stosay." A tiny voice crept forward from the group of students. Again, there was a low growl, a motionless stare, followed by a cheerful reply.

"Yes my child" the student was young Marci of 7 years. She was already scared but felt the need to ask a question.

"Now that Bazetar was free, did he go on and kill everybody?" Stosay chuckled at the innocent question.

"No child. The god Attel sensed the Troll King's escape after he was already in the Castillo Morta. He created an Orb Shield that kept him trapped in the upper section of the castle. No one could penetrate it so he stopped making Trowcans since the provisions were only enough for a few. That means that the god of the dead simply left his old prison for a much nicer one."

The State Of Things

Sadanasia walked down a long corridor leading to a pair of large doors. She reached for a door handle with her, now gray and scaly arm. The door opened smoothly and she arrogantly strutted in. She was still wearing the same black dress she wore the night her parents were killed. There on the floor was Sarre, her twin sister sitting against a wall. The room was dark only allowing moon light to offer any relief from it. Sadanasia had no problem seeing. Her eyes now held permanent night vision gifted to her by her king. She looked down at her pitiful sister who was lifting her head to meet Sadanasia. She let out a smug chuckle.

"Get up." She lightly kicked Sarre's leg with a heeled foot. Sarre quietly stood up and tried to focus on her sister but could not see her. She was restrained by chains bolted to the center of the floor.

"How do you fair sister?" Sarre drooped her head remaining silent.

"Answer your queen!" nothing but Sadanasia's own voice echoed in the room. Sarre lifted her head again.

"My king and queen, mother and father are dead. I have no allegiance to you." Sarre said defiantly knowing these words would greatly upset her twin. What she did not know was what her response would be. Still shrouded in darkness, a low growl was heard coming from Sadanasia's direction.

"I am your queen now!" suddenly her face was right in Sarre's, moonlight revealing her new altered form. Her face too was covered in scales and out of her scalp rose long curving spikes instead of hair. Her teeth were now fangs and her finger tips ended in sharp nails. Sarre screamed and then quickly covered her mouth still taking in her sister's new appearance.

"What is wrong my twin? Do you not approve? Am I not more beautiful now than I ever was before?" she walked closer to the only window in the room where her whole body was in the light. Sadanasia held out her hands as her gown began to move on its own. The clasp over her chest became undone revealing itself to be two long fingers ending in talons. The dress completely opened up into two leathery wings attached to her back. Sarre gasped at the sight of her completely nude twin. Sadanasia's stared into Sarre's eyes with a menacing grin on her face.

"The gown was given to me by the new king. It is befitting the most important being in his existence. He showers me with all kinds of gifts and finery. I simply don't know what to do with it all." She chuckled and walked casually to the large window to view her kingdom with her wings still extended. Sarre watched her silently while thinking of what to say to her.

"Sadanasia, look what you have become. Look at what he has made you. He is the god of the dead. We all learned about his crimes as children. Where do you think you'll end up siding with him?"

"Here is where I'll end up sister, ruling a vast kingdom with a husband who loves and respects me. Who will never take me for granted or make me do things that are beneath my standing! I know that you are jealous of me. What can I say? The better sister won."

"You are delusional! He has infected your mind!"

"Enough!" Sadanasia shouted in two voices, her own and a deep rumbling one. She growled as her eyes began to glow brighter.

"You will remain chained there, until all we can do is scrape off what is left of your rotting corpse. The same fate awaits Abel and Xenon. Somehow the twits managed to evade our forces." The wings tucked neatly back into place forming a dress. Sarre was unaware that her brothers had escaped. She finally had a glimmer of hope in her endless torment.

"Good night dear sister." The door slowly closed on her piercing eyes and evil grin. Sarre fell to the floor, sobbing till daylight returned.

On the Gold beach of Tridom there walked a herd of giant River Bulls, ill-tempered animals the size of a house. The bulls had just emerged from the harbor and were making their way up to the grassy hills past the palm tree barrier. A single path cutting through had been trotted for ages by all kinds of local wildlife. As they made their way past, one of them stopped and raised its long furry ears. A miniscule sound came from the heavy vegetation within the palms. One of the older bulls snorted an alarm call causing the herd of 30 beasts to panic. They ran clear of the tree barrier and behind them, in fast pursuit, was a slender figure wearing a hood and scarf concealing their face. The stampeding animals were extremely fast for their size, trampling all the foliage beneath them. The person in pursuit jumped into the air grasping the branch of a tree and swinging down to a large bull. The hooded person held on the animal's enormous craggy horns and stabbed it in the center of its skull with a sword. The animal moaned painfully, still taking a few steps before it collapsed. A cloud of dust surrounded Nyka as she pulled off her hood and scarf. She was breathing rapidly, trying to catch her breath while admiring her prize. The River Bull was a very difficult animal to kill, and now she was one of the few who could. Out of the dust cloud appeared another River Bull with its horns aimed right for her. Nyka froze completely caught off guard. Then there was another loud moan and the creature fell over dead. The momentum of the charge made the brute slide for a few feet. Another scarfed figure emerged from the dust and stood on the bull's ribs. It was her father.

“Father! I didn’t need any help.” Nwendor jumped of the carcass’s while retracting his bloody blades back into his fingers.

“I see that now. There was absolutely no reason for me to come and save your life just now. Was there?” he looked to her as she disregarded his assistance.

“I was supposed to be on my own. How am I supposed to learn what I need to survive if you keep coming to rescue me?”

“My girl I am sorry to upset you, but this is parenting. You should feel lucky I am always around to maintain your safety.”

“Oh, sure I am the lucky one that always gets coddled by you. What about the 5? Why don’t you go to them for a change?” Nwendor uncrossed his arms his pupils formed vertical slits.

“That had better be the last time you disrespect me. Do you understand?” he had his finger in Nyka’s face and glared at her with his inhuman eyes. He began to walk the trail leading towards the Gold Beach. Nyka was shocked by what she had said to her father. A strong feeling of guilt overcame her since she knew he was just trying to protect her.

The 5 were her half brothers and sisters. All were Nwendor’s children he had had after Irlan’s death. He had taken many mistresses trying to alleviate the pain of his loss. Of all the flings he had there resulted 5 children, 2 girls and 3 boys. All of whom were provided for but lacked the presence of a father. He wanted no part in there upbringing as he only cared for Nyka. They were raised by the forked tongues of their scorned mothers who constantly let them know how their father had abandoned them. They were constantly reminded how Tridom would be theirs if Nwendor and Nyka were gone. They were all trained in the art of combat by the best the Yaga had to offer for all their lives. United in their hatred for their father, they pledged to destroy him and their sister.

She ran after her father trying to catch up to apologize.

Once she reached the beach she caught the view of by Nwendor's back and the sight of approaching warships. They flew the Kreshant banner as they entered the protected harbor.

"Abel." crept out of Nyka's lips while clutching her hands together. Nwendor turned to her with a look of dissatisfaction.

"We need to gather the council. Something has happened." They ran off together in the direction of the palace with the speed of an arrow. Word spread rapidly to all the corners of the island. The Yaga gathered into huge crowds at the Central Arena. Marcus arrived without an escort, ever the lone standing mountain. He sat straight and silent with his trusty sword resting on his laps. His helmet hid the look of concern as it made a shadow around the exposed areas of his face. His caught the movement of Nwendor climbing into his seat. Nwendor nodded his head to the lesser god but he remained stoic as ever. A long procession of royal guards marched from the landing zone on the Gold Beach, through the palm barrier, over to the Central Arena. The two lesser gods sat in their thrones trying to figure out what was going on. They were both certain that this was not an attack because of the lack of fighting formations. Migus' throne was empty since he had not cared enough to be torn from his mistresses of the night. Matiun approached with his old arms raised.

"Great and mighty kings of..."

"Why are you here Sagen?" Marcus cut right to the point as dry as ever towards Abel. Matiun bowed and stepped off to the side.

"We are on the run my lords."

"From what? Surely you have the means to defend yourself." Nwendor gestured to the army numbering 10,000 and the ships visible from the harbor.

"Bazetar has returned!" hundreds of gasps filled the air.

"His hordes are running unchecked throughout Boe Chantra. Soon there will be no one left alive." Said Abel with great urgency.

"Impossible, he was defeated, entombed, how is he back Prince Abel?" asked Marcus.

"My sister freed him!" yelled little Xenon from behind his big brother.

"She killed my mom and dad!" Xenon broke out into tears.

"Yes my lords. What my baby brother says is true. Sadanasia has betrayed us and all of humanity. My parents are dead, the majority of our forces have been destroyed along with the country. The armies are endless and continue to expand outwards in order to leave Boe Chantra an uninhabited wasteland."

"Why do you approach us now, Sagen?" asked Nwendor.

"My lords we traveled here in search of safety and a place to prepare for the re-conquest of our home. We also came to beg for your help." Nwendor and Marcus gave each other a glance and looked back at Abel.

"You would have us commit our forces to lands they've never been to. A land where they will probably meet their end?" asked Nwendor.

"Young prince, we have peace here. What goes on in other lands does not concern us. You think the Yaga want to go somewhere far away to die?"

"King Marcus, the Trowcans will continue to consume all the land. Eventually they will find themselves here at your doorstep. Right now we can combine forces, let us stay and we will help you repel them."

"You speak as if you know something is already on its way."

"King Nwendor, it is only a matter of time. The more we wait the bigger his armies grow." Nwendor again looked to Marcus again, who gave him a silent nod.

"Before we even consider committing our forces to your cause, we must be certain the Trowcans have designs for our land. The Siren are a race of ocean dwellers that are friends to the Yaga. We'll ask them to send a detail to investigate Kreshant's port. Whenever they return, you will have your answer."

"Nwendor..."

"Sagen, for the meantime you may anchor your ships and make camp for your army. I'm sure those fighting have lost a lot and need rest."

"Yes King Nwendor." Abel bowed his head, not happy with waiting but still happy that he and his people were taken in. A loud singing voice came within earshot of all in the arena.

"What did I miss?" asked Migus while leaping into his throne as Abel gave shouted an order and the army went to work.

Many days later, a group of Siren were swimming towards the port of Kreshant. The Siren were humanoid but with long eel like tails instead of legs. They carried harpoons in their hands and shields on their backs. Massive domesticated sharks that were trained over the millennia pulled them most of the way. Once they were close enough the Siren left their mounts and stealthily swam into the port. There they saw an armada of transport ships that would carry the Trowcan Southern Army to Tridom. They were being prepared for an invasion. Thousands upon thousands of Trowcans were waiting to board the ships that were more like barges since they lacked sails. Long black chains reached from the ships to the surface of the water. There they were attached to the armor of bone plated fish almost the size of the ship itself. The Siren were not familiar with this species and attributed their existence to Bazetar's black magic.

Those mega bone jawed fish were going to pull them all the way to Tridom. The Siren had seen enough and silently gestured to each other that it was time to leave. As they began to move, one of the mega fish spotted them and let out a low resounding roar that hurt the Siren's ears and caused the one closest to the fish to collapse. The Trowcans were alerted to their presence and began raining arrows and spears at them. The Detail of Siren dodged and weaved but many of them were struck down. Of the original 20 only 4 made it to the shark transports. They swam in desperation to warn Tridom.

There they were on Gold Beach, studying each other. Nyka was perched in a crouching position on the sandy shore while Abel swam in the clear waters. She wore her usual attire except for her armor which was left at the palace. She couldn't help but stare at the Sagen prince as his muscles flexed with every stroke and paddle. Her admiration was interrupted when he let out a shout from where he was swimming. The water around him became white with violent movement as he struggled to make for the shore. Nyka snapped to her feet and ran to aid the prince. They met up in knee deep water.

"What is it! What is it!" Abel yelled in desperation.

"Let me see. Calm down!"

"Get it off! Get it off!" Nyka put her hands on his chiseled abdomen and ran her fingers to the affected area. There hanging off his side was a Lamprey measuring 3 feet in length.

"Eww, that is unfortunate." Nyka said with concern.

"What! What do you mean? Get it off of me!"

"Well I could but, the creature is already a part of you. Once they latch on they slowly work their way to your brain, and then they take over completely. Turning you into a zombie."

"What! There must be something we can..." Abel looked down at the wriggling, snake like fish and began to feel sick.

Every movement the creature made pulled on his skin as it tried to get to his blood.

"There's another one!" Nyka exclaimed while pointing at his shoulder.

"Where!" as he turned to see the other Lamprey, Nyka grabbed and pulled the one at his side so quickly that all he could do was yelp in a high pitch. She began to laugh so hard tears came out of her eyes. Abel saw that there was no other Lamprey on him and gave her a look of embarrassment. He had his hands on his hips and took in all the humiliation as Nyka began to snort and hold her sides. He kicked the wriggling fish back into the water and wiped the area of skin it had bitten.

"What is wrong prince? Can't take a joke?" she began to poke his stomach playfully with both index fingers which, even though he was built like a rock, was painful since she possessed her father's strength. He shuddered as every poke felt like a light punch.

"Stop!" he yelled as he grabbed both of her wrists. She started to calm down and with a bit of laughter still left in her said.

"You would do good to unhand me sir." He gave her a sly smile and made a quick motion to trap her in his embrace. Nyka, ever faster and stronger than he was, simply dodged the move and countered with a sweep that put him on his back. He let out a groan as her foot rested on his neck. He looked up at her slender figure lit by the sun.

"I yield my princess. You have bested me." He said under strain as he could not remove her foot even if he wanted to.

"Rise Sagen." She moved her boot off of him and walked away a few feet before facing him with her hands still at her hips. Abel began brushing off the golden sand from his skin.

"You know, this island could be one of the richest countries in the world if you began to smelt this sand into ingots."

"The beach is sacred to the Yaga. It is legend that the first to arrive here were the richest merchants ever. Their ships were laden with gold and they were looking for a place to invest their already infinite riches. They soon found out that the island was uninhabited so they prepared to leave but the overloaded ships had run aground. The group of merchants and their crew had to find a way to build new ships to return to their homes. After the weeks of work turned to years, the stranded ships and the gold they carried were pulverized into sand by the ocean. Those who remained eventually became the Yaga who pass this story down generations."

"Huh... Well that was a great story, but maybe they should've continued trying to escape. Think of all the security they would've had now to protect themselves from all manners of surprise attack!" he lunged at Nyka who saw the move coming a mile away only this time she didn't dodge and let Abel put his muscular arms around her. He was oozing with confidence not knowing that Nyka was simply holding back to allow him this tiny victory. He held her in his arms and softened his grip as they stared into each other's eyes. He was breathing heavily with an open smiling mouth. He began to lean in for a kiss, while she was lost in his gaze. When he was mere millimeters from her lips she turned away.

"I am sorry Prince Abel. I should have exercised more self-control."

"You have nothing to apologize for Nyka." Their embrace began to loosen when a harpoon landed at their feet sticking out of the sand. Nyka reacted instantly jumping in the air rolling, and then landing with two throwing daggers in her hands. Abel looked to the water where there stood a group of Sirens.

The three kings of Tridom arrived at the Gold Beach to meet the race from the sea. There were 6 guards flanking 2

Sirens situated in the middle. It was their king and his son who was learning how to govern so he could eventually take over. King Bagrae began to sign with his arms at the leaders now standing in the waist high water. Possessing only a primitive lung the Sirens could not speak with air breathers, so they used a form of sign language to communicate. The Yaga and the gods understood the exchange perfectly.

"The Trowcans Southern Army coming. It appears you were right young prince."

"How many are coming?" Abel asked Nwendor.

"Thousands on giant barges filled to capacity with soldiers, pulled by wretched sea monsters."

"We must prepare. The Trowcan armies are vicious, and merciless. What will we do?" asked Abel.

"The Siren say they will help destroy the barges. Apparently they do not like sea monsters in their oceans." Marcus gave a thankful gesture to King Bargae who then he left with his escort back into the sea.

"My lords, now that we know they are coming we really should…"

"Pick a leader!" Migus shouted while barely arriving and interrupting Matiun.

"I vote myself as the obvious choice. I am way more intelligent and better looking than Marcus and Nwendor, sorry boys." Migus looked at his fellow king and grinned.

"I am the obvious choice. I am the strongest and will lead with brute strength." Exclaimed Marcus as he hit his chest once with his fist.

"I believe I am the only one for the job, but we must decide soon. I declare a Divine Contest." Everyone on the beach gasped except Abel and his people who had no idea what that was.

“Nwendor! You bring us much excitement. I can’t wait.” Migus walked away confidently.

“What is a Divine Contest?” Abel asked Nyka.

“The Central Arena is used to resolve differences between the 3 kingdoms of Tridom. The 3 lesser gods will battle each other to decide who leads our forces. Fun right?” Nyka walked away with a smile as the entire island lit up with excitement to attend the bout.

That night the Arena seats were filled to capacity. Those who did not get a seat, stood in any vacant spot. Matiun was chosen to provide a statement to the masses to let them know what was at stake. He took position in the center and spoke with his old yet projecting voice.

“Welcome all.” The crowd silenced as his voice echoed in all directions.

“As all of you may have heard. We are all in great danger. The Trowcans are preparing a fleet that will arrive in a very short time. We must prepare for the coming invasion. As you all know these corrupt beings want nothing more than to consume each and every one of you. Your women, children, elderly, and even pets are not safe.” Murmurs filled the arena.

“Our lords will now commence in a brawl known as Devine Contest to decide who will lead us into battle. Last god standing will be the victor.” The crowd erupted in cheers as the 3 gods walked out of their respective doorways leading to their palaces. Marcus walked out with his Sun Piercer sword resting on his shoulder. He wore a barbute helmet, a white tunic with the image of a black flying dragon on his right breast, with his pants and heavy leather boots. Nwendor walked out wearing leather armor, which allowed for faster movement, a long scarf hanging from his back, and metal greaves. He had 2 war axes attached to his back in an “X” configuration. Migus walked out waving to the crowds and blowing them kisses. He was wearing full chain mail, a white and black tunic, topped off with a gold, jewel encrusted crown. In his hands was the 11 point spear crafted by Relo. The cheers continued on as the 3 made their way to the center of the arena. Their thrones had been removed leaving a wide open space. Matiun ran at a quick pace to exit the zone of combat as the 3 stared each other down.

"My lords I am so glad we got to come here to engage in a bout of politicking." Migus was gloating as he spun his spear in his hands.

"Migus, I was hoping this day would come soon. I owe you."

"Nwendor are you talking about the time I zapped you? That was ages ago. Does it still hurt? I am that powerful you know."

"Enough of this. We are here to pick a winner not bicker like school children!" Marcus shot a fireball at Nwendor and lunged at Migus. Migus and Nwendor jumped out of the way but Marcus was able to grab hold of Migus' tunic. Marcus tried to slam him on the ground with one arm but a jolt of electricity surged through him. Migus jumped away and was sent hurling towards the arena wall by a double kick from Nwendor. As he flew through the air Migus corrected himself to where his feet hit the wall. He then propelled himself back towards Nwendor with his spearhead leading in horizontal flight. Nwendor used a telekinetic pulse to stop Migus right before he skewered him. Migus flipped backwards and landed on his feet. A trickle of blood ran down his nose. Nwendor was lowering his arm when he sensed a fireball coming towards him. He tried to dodge, but it caught his shoulder knocking him over and leaving it flaming. Nwendor patted it furiously to stop the fire when a solid uppercut from Marcus sent him flying in an arc till he hit the floor. Migus jumped in the air and was able to stab Marcus in the thigh with his spear. Marcus roared in pain, and then backhanded Migus across the face, stunning him. He then lifted his leg to stomp him into the ground when a bolt of lightning left Migus' finger tips and hit Marcus in the face. As he convulsed, Nwendor tackled Migus to the ground ending the lightning attack. He stood over Migus and tried to take a swipe at his face with his blades. Migus caught his wrists and the two continued to struggle.

"You are strong fallen god, but not impervious to me!" Migus' eyes began to glow a pale blue while his grip tightened. Nwendor only had a second to think before thousands of volts surged through his body. As he shook violently from the attack a column of steady fire hit both of them, sending them careening towards the arena wall. They lodged into the wall like boulders from a catapult. Marcus lowered his arm and held out his sword. His leg healed quickly after the spear was pulled from his thigh. The gods were all blessed with quick healing so he knew the two were not defeated. At the same time both Migus and Nwendor shot out of the wall at incredible speed. Migus, so focused on Marcus did not see that Nwendor was right over him with his blades aiming for him. The blades stabbed him in the back coming out his chest. Migus still had his momentum but lost control of his trajectory. He reached Marcus but was holding his wound. Marcus back fisted Migus sending him flying out of the way. Over Migus' appeared the burned and bludgeoned Nwendor, still with all his speed and both hands outstretched ending in 8 blades. Nwendor's foot collided with Marcus' face knocking him back to the ground. Nwendor stood over the downed titan of a man and also stabbed his chest. Both Migus and Marcus were on the ground clutching their chests and only Nwendor was on his feet. The crowd cheered riotously at the results of the Divine Contest. Migus and Marcus sat up while still hugging their bloody wounds. Matiun raced out and bowed to the new general.

"Supreme Commander Nwendor!" he gestured to the victor and began clapping. Among the spectators sat Nyka. She was clapping with excitement for her father.

"Hello Princess." The voice of Abel spoke in her ear and jumped into the seat next to her.

"What are you doing here? We need to stop meeting like this. Altor will be very upset."

"Let him be upset. I thought you'd be delighted to see me"

"Well I'm not. So that means you can go now."

"I don't believe you, and these flowers I picked personally for you also disagree." He held out a bouquet of flowers picked from the palace garden and held them out to her. She smiled with joy as she too them from his hands. She thanked Abel and gave them a gentle smell.

"They are so beautiful. Thank you." She didn't care if they were from the palace garden. It was the gesture that brought her delight.

"Princess, beauty springs from the ground in the form of these flowers, but beauty springs forth from you in rays of brilliant radiance." He held his smile and starred into her light brown eyes.

"Wow Prince Abel, that had to be the tritest thing ever said to me." She broke out laughing.

"Really? I worked on that line for hours. Did you hear the whole thing? Do you want me to repeat it again?"

"No, please no. I can only take so much." She continued laughing and Abel looked out to the arena in defeat.

"I'm sorry, I'm sorry. It was wonderful. I appreciate the effort." Her laughter calmed as she brushed her long white hair out of her face.

"So, do you think the other two will do as they're told?" he gestured to Marcus and Migus.

"Yes. They have to. The Divine Contest is a very serious

matter and even Migus honors it.

"Migus. Well I'm glad he didn't win. He is way too free spirited. It is unbecoming of a military leader. Marcus would've been fine. He is serious and strong. I guess either him or Nwendor would've made good candidates." He turned to Nyka who nodded in agreement while sniffing her flowers again.

"My lord I have to go."

"Wait. Nyka"

"It was nice seeing you again. Thank you for the flowers." she stood and hurried off leaving the lovelorn Abel behind. He sat back down and rested his head in his hands contemplating his next move. The two children that splashed water on him before were pointing and laughing at him.

The following day, the Island leadership set up a meeting. There they would discuss strategies to defend Tridom. They sat at a long wooden table and all looked to Nwendor who was quiet. His eyes were not focused on the present, but were lost in the past somewhere with his wife.

"My lord, We must begin." Abel said. It was like talking to a statue. He looked to Matiun who promptly stood and walked over to Nwendor. He spoke softly.

"My lord, Are you well?"

"Matiun, you are to be the architect of the island defenses." Nwendor's voice pierced the air and all the others in the council began to converse.

"Quiet all of you commanded Zeto, high counselor of the Yaga." The council silenced.

"Matiun. We have only two points where an army can make it ashore. The Gold Beach and the Bone River. Everywhere else is protected by steep cliffs." Said Marcus. The Bone River was a long corridor leading to the ocean where ages ago there was once a mighty river. Now it was a barren passageway with cliffs on each side making for a perfect choke point.

"The Yaga will defend Gold Beach. It is our place of worship. We will water it with the blood of the invaders."

"Good Zeto. I along with Marcus and Migus will assist in repulsing them." Nwendor and Zeto nodded to each other.

"Abel I will leave you in command of your army. Soldiers need to follow someone they trust. You will be tasked with holding the Bone River pass."

"Yes commander." The council stood and gave their proper respects before going off to their duties. Nyka walked up to her father.

"Where will I be father?"

"You will be here, away from all the brutality coming our way."

"No! I want to be in the action. I need to help. I am way stronger than any of the soldiers on this Island."

"Come Matiun, we will see to the defenses of the beach." Marcus' voice overpowered all others in the room as they walked out.

"My daughter..." Nwendor tried to give a reason as to why she could not participate but couldn't think of one. Her persistent, angry brown eyes stared right at him. She was an adult, a skilled fighter, and a deadly killer. He softly closed his eyes and took a deep breath.

"Okay, I know you are not a little girl anymore. I shouldn't keep holding you back." Nyka stared at him waiting for him to finish his thought.

"You will help defend the Bone River. We expect the attack from there will be a smaller contingent of the main army." Nyka yelled in glee, first clapping her hands then hugging her father. He smiled in her warm embrace and she saluted him before running off to prepare for battle. The room was now quiet. Nwendor placed his palms on a map of Tridom as he studied it. A singing voice could be heard coming nearer and then the door burst open.

"What did I miss?" asked Migus

5

"So you see my children, the tiny island of Tridom was bustling with movement. Only little children and the elderly were allowed to take refuge while the rest were expected to fight." Stosay's soulless mask moved slowly from side to side gauging the reactions of the students.

"Why was Migus always late?" asked Crux.

"Well the lesser god was great at fighting and seducing women and not much else." Stosay walked past the boy with his hands behind his back. He noticed that Beth, his student of 10 years old, was laying on her stomach and playing with a piece of string.

"Beth, you need to pay attention to the lesson. Sit up please." She ignored the teacher and the rest of the students remained silent. They all stared at the girl who was now moving her feet forward and backwards while humming a tune. The other students now in shock stared at Stosay's smiling mask. A low audible growl exited his mouth hole and filled their ears with fright.

"Dear you need to sit up and pay attention." The little girl sat up facing her teacher.

"I don't have to do anything. You're ugly and your teaching is dumb." The girl stood, walked over to a table Stosay reserved for statuettes of various figures and started playing with them. She was also humming purposely trying to disrupt class further. Stosay walked over to the girl slowly and grabbed her arm with his mitten. His grasp was hard enough to hurt but light enough not to leave a mark.

"Hey! Leave me..." Stosay turned the girl to where she was looking into the black eye voids in his mask. He leaned in closer to her face and the same growl was heard again. The little girl was petrified with fear. A feeling of darkness emanated outwards from Stosay as the candles began to pulse. Then, a loud ring filled the classroom. The parents of the children had arrived to take them home. Stosay's slow predatory movements were instantly changed to cheerful energetic ones. He led the students to the door and handed them off to their parents.

"May I have a word Mr. Helt?"

"What is it? We have to get going."

"I assure you that it will only take a bit of your time." Stosay looked to little Beth, and then back to her father.

"Bethany here is not listening to the history lesson. She does not respond to simple commands either."

"Look Master Stosay, the entire teaching endeavor is your trade, not mine. If you can't handle her, then find a new profession. Good Day to you." Mr. Helt walked off holding Beth's hand. She turned to face her teacher and grinned smugly. Stosay stood there as still as a boulder and growled under his mask in the frigid snow.

The following day the children waited in the snow again. They continued to complain about the cold and how Stosay was taking too long. Then the conversation shifted to mocking their servants and then each other. Again the story sayer appeared suddenly, scaring his students who were shy one girl. The class went inside and warmed themselves by the fireplace. Stosay opened the Boe Chantra history book to the page where they left off.

"Where is Beth master Stosay?" asked Crux

"I wouldn't know. She may not be feeling well at the moment. Now, everyone sit down." With his voice in a deep rumble, Stosay calmed the students, who listened immediately in order to avoid a repeat of the darkness.

The Invasion Of Tridom

Tridom, once a lush paradise was now an intimidating fortress. The Gold Beach and the Bone River Pass were teaming with soldiers. Only the Bone River had defensive structures built on it since the beach was considered too precious a sight to dig up. The Yaga were very skilled warriors with the knowledge of combat passed on through the ages. All wore head dresses adorned with long colorful feathers from a bird species called Tetherwings, that were considered sacred. Their armor was made of bone plates from local wildlife and the Shard Club was their preferred weapon. It was a long wooden paddle with sharp metal shards sticking outwards. Spears were also used, as well as the bow and arrow for ranged attacks. Abel and his army were traditionally clad in suits of steel armor with swords and pikes. They had already received warning that the Trowcan Southern army was almost there.

Nyka was walking over to stand with Abel's army when she was grabbed by the arm.

"Where are you going Nyka?"

"Altor? I am going to my position with the army. What is wrong?"

"I forbid your involvement in this affair. Your place is with me, not among the island brutes."

"My place is assuring the survival of Tridom. What has gotten into you?" she pulled her arm away and began walking.

"Don't think I don't know about your private sessions with the prince. You milady are a liar!" the people in the vicinity halted their activities and stared at the couple.

"Don't think you know anything because you do not. I don't belong by anyone's side. I go where I choose and that is final." Altor balled his fist fanaticizing about hitting her. He knew she could easily pulverize him so he just stood there grinding his teeth.

"Good day to you sir." Nyka walked away towards the formations of Abel's army.

As she walked away from her suitor she noticed that all the sound in the area stopped. She looked around and all the people were frozen in various poses of everyday life. She pulled out her sword, a long thin blade given to her by her father. As she looked around an enormous figure materialized in front of her. She jumped back, her sword at the ready, but strangely felt no sense of danger from the hulking Aires standing before her.

"Nyka, my granddaughter, it is good to finally meet you. You may put that blade away." She did exactly as she was told and sheathed the long sword.

"Grandfather?"

"Yes. We are not allowed to interfere in the destinies of mortals but times are dire and we are allowed one visit. I have brought you this." He held out his hand which held a glowing purple egg. It was the size of a watermelon and weighed the same. Nyka grabbed it with both her hands. Once the egg felt the heat from her hands it began to crack. Chittering came from within the shaking egg and then 2 wings popped out. They were followed by 4 clawed legs. The creature's head poked through revealing a small spotted gray dragon. Nyka cooed at the animal and it responded by rubbing its neck and head against her arm.

"She is yours. She will accompany you on your journey. I will be watching you my dear." Aires dematerialize into nothing before Nyka could thank him or ask questions. The bustling started up again as if nothing had happened. She looked at her dog sized dragon while it panted and stared at her.

"You're covered in dots and spots. I will name you Dotoria." She placed her on the ground seeing that the newly hatched Dotoria was already able to walk without a problem. She followed Nyka closely sniffing everything along the way to the Bone River.

Nwendor also had a pet he named Pykas. It was a rare black and beige Battle Hound. Pykas was bigger than a horse and had retractable catlike nails on his front paws. Nwendor and a select few Yagan warriors mounted the Battle Hounds and used them as cavalry or were left unmounted to attack at will. Pykas was fiercely loyal and distrusted all who came close to Nwendor except for Nyka. Nwendor rode the hound over to Gold Beach and dismounted. He walked over to the Yagan warriors as they hid in the palm barrier. Their war paint was black, green, yellow, and brown blending in perfectly with the vegetation. All the Yaga were here filling the only passage into the interior of the island. Cliffs and boulders flanked their position on both sides. It was a very easy area to defend. A loud horn blasted forth in the distance. The warning call was heard loud and clearly by all the defenders. The Trowcan Southern army had arrived.

For hours the defenders of Gold Beach watched the troop barges get pulled as far as the mega fish could before the water got too shallow. Long oars came out from openings on the sides of the vessels and rowed them the rest of the way. The boxy shape of the barges made them sluggish to row, but allowed for maximum transportation of troops. A gangway was lowered from the bow tip allowing the Trowcans to disembark rapidly. Within an hour a Trowcan army of thousands held the beach. The defenders were absolutely quiet as the order was given for archers. The Trowcan line spanned the entire beach, from cliff to cliff, and was ten soldiers deep. The front two lines were made up of the giant, heavily armored Sav-trows. The Trowcans were weary of the silence. They knew that the defenders were hidden somewhere in the heavy foliage. Only the waves lapping the golden sand made any noise.

"Trowcans! Advance!" commanded General Forred. Forred was a matriarch in her past life. She was one who was known for lying, negligence, and the manipulation of her family so they would do her biding. Many of them suffered, with multiple casualties in her lifetime. She resented her family for not attending her funeral or praying for her as her soul putrefied in the Plains of Sorrow. The Trowcans did not have different genders, just uniform vessels filled with damned souls. Hers was placed in a body and made into a general because of her great skills.

The Trowcans marched forward carefully trying to listen for any sign of life. The long whistle of a sole arrow left the palms and hit a Trowcan right between its eyes. It fell to the sand as more arrows began to fall from the sky. The Trowcan army countered the attack by forming themselves into a shield wall. The Sav-trows' heavy metal tower shields easily protected them from the front and the round wooden shields of the regulars were held above their heads. Many of them died pinned to the sand but most were able to absorb the arrow shower.

"Men and women of the Yaga! It is time to save your home! Charge!" the entire Yagan line rolled forward towards the Trowcans. The distance from the palm barrier to the Trowcan front line was 300ft. Nwendor ran ahead of the army who were not fast enough to keep up with his pace. Trowcan arrows flew at him but he held a steel kite shield that covered most of his body and his legs were armored from the knee down. At a full sprint he crashed into a Sav-Trow sending the one ton monster rolling into the soldiers behind it. He was surrounded by the enemy. He took a battle axe in each hand and began hacking them to pieces. He was too fast to hit and too strong to do any damage to. He cleaved a head in half with an axe and then threw it to a Sav-trow killing it. He threw the other axe hitting a Trowcan regular in the chest. He raised both hands letting out a short telekinetic pulse that sent 10 Trowcans flying into their ranks. Nwendor extended his blades while an enormous crash was heard as the rest of the army reached the Trowcan line. Further down the formation was Migus who was spearing the invaders left and right. He raised his right hand as bolt of lightning struck his fingers, then began electrocuting the Trowcans around him. He lowered his arm and began attacking with his spear which had a spearhead on one end and a spikey ball at the base, along with other spikes giving it eleven points. Even further down walked Marcus casually. He had his sword at his side and his left palm pointed at the Trowcan army. A column of fire blasted through the enemy ranks charring countless bodies. A group of Sav-trows charged at him. He stopped one dead in its tracks by grabbing its throat then easily ripping it out. Another Sav-trow was sliced in half, shield, armor, and all, by his mighty sword. Fire shot forth from his hand making the remaining Sav-trows walking bonfires. The Trowcans continued to fall as the Yagan army pushed them back into the sea. A loud howl was heard coming from the palm barrier. It was Pykas and the rest of his pack of battle hounds charging for the Trowcan line. They were careful not to trample their own and jumped over the collapsing Sav-trow line. The Trowcan regulars were given gruesome maulings by the frenzied Battle Hounds. Pykas' tan snout was covered in Trowcan blood as his claws tore through the enemy with great ease. Those who tried to escape the carnage by climbing on their barges were picked off by bolts and arrows shot from the Yagan archers who had moved closer. As the Trowcans at the rear entered the water harpoons began to impale them as the Siren soldiers emerged. The mega fish still chained to the barges were easy pickings for the agile Sirens who knew now that they had to keep their distance. The Trowcan Southern Army was completely surrounded.

At the Bone River, Nyka waited with the Sagen formation. Their defensive line stretched from one rocky wall to the other. They were 3 soldiers deep, with spears in the front, swords behind, and further back, spaced 10ft behind the line were archers.

A small segment of the southern army was sent to secure the Bone River, but it still outnumbered the Sagen forces 3 to 1. The Trowcans marched towards the army and stopped 50ft from them. Unlike the gold beach there would be no surprise here. The invaders began banging on their shields and letting loose with taunts. The Sagens held firm watching the army's every movement. A horn blasted and the order to attack was given by a captain under Forred. The mass of bodies crashed into Sagen shields and spears. Nyka walked out into the fray and heard a voice cry out.

"Princess stay right here! It is not safe!" Abel still had the body of a drooping Trowcan on his sword. Nyka rolled her eyes as she uncoiled her whip and drew her sword. The whip ended in a small steel dart and she used it to stab the eyes of the Trowcans as well as other tender places. She would wrap it around their necks and pull them towards her to finish them with her sword. In an instant she dropped 10 Trowcans while Abel killed 4. He looked to her in astonishment and she nodded to him and smiled. Dotoria still at Nyka's side ran past her into the enemy ranks. Nyka tried to stop her but she disappeared into the Trowcan horde. A flash of white light was seen bursting from the mass as Dotoria's original size of a medium dog grew to the size of a rhino. She began breathing a purple flame that incinerated all it touched. From the top of the cliff came formations of archers from both sides that were hidden in the vegetation. Arrows were shot into the Trowcans who had yet to make it to the Sagen shield wall. The archers were protected by their elevated position and picked off the Trowcans with pin point accuracy. The Trowcans were pushed back towards their landing craft. They retreated with the pain of hunger holding no value in the face of a second death. To their dismay, the barges were already destroyed by the Sirens. The detachment of the Trowcan Southern Army was completely destroyed.

The mop up was going smoothly. The Yagan army

suffered minimal casualties, which was unheard of when battling the Trowcans. All was not well with the Siren King though . His son, the prince Gat had been slain by a Trowcan spear. The spear head was thrown from the top of a barge and entered his gill slits as he clashed with another Trowcan. The father held his young heir in his long thin arms and mourned. He looked up at the lords of Tridom and began to sign his utter contempt for them. The lords understood that he was in pain and let him carry on his tirade. When he was done he let them know that they would never help them again and disappeared along with his soldiers into the sea. The Yagan soldiers were finishing off the wounded invaders with sword and spears. Suddenly, a lone dead Trowcan stood with its entrails hanging out of an open cavity in its abdomen. It raised its head and opened its eyes revealing two black voids.

"You think we are done here?" a low voice could be heard by all followed by a chuckle.

"The magic of these gods won't hold me forever. I will return with a bigger army which I will be personally commanding. Your victory is meaningless. All you managed to do was buy a little bit of time." Bazetar let out another chuckle followed by a hum that grew louder. The dead Trowcan began to convulse violently before exploding into a million pieces. All who had ducked for cover rose to their feet cautiously while looking at the smoking crater.

"That was him." Migus looked to Marcus and Nwnedor.

"Yes, I believe that was the god of the dead. I think we made him angry. What do you recommend Nwendor?" asked Marcus.

"Let us meet at my palace."

"My palace is better! More roomy and far more luxurious." Migus smiled at his fellow rulers still covered in Trowcan blood.

"Fine, we will meet at Migus' palace to go over our options." Two massive fires were lit to burn the mountains of Trowcan dead that night. All the leaders met at Migus' palace where he made it a point to have them all be waited on and pampered during their visit. All except for Marcus and Nwendor were dressed in white robes. The lesser gods did not find Migus' lavish party appealing. The guests were given fine wine and delicious delicacies served on the finest dining ware on the island. Many could not eat as the horrors of battle were still fresh on their minds.

"Enough with the fineries." Marcus slammed his goblet of wine on the table stopping the music and conversation.

"War is coming to our shores again. Only this time it will be the entire Trowcan army! I will not sit idly by while they come and consume us all. I will not put my family through that. Migus! This is not Attel's realm, no matter how much you would attempt to make it so." Migus had a woman on his lap with her hand on his chest. He gestured with his head to the woman that it was time to go. She quickly stood and blew him a kiss as she left.

"Okay my lord, clearly you have no notion of unwinding. What is the plan then?"

Abel stood from his seat commanding everyone's attention.

"The beast resides in my family's castle. For now he is trapped by the Orb Shield, which means we can hold him there before he is unleashed on the world again." There were loud murmurs all around.

"Sagen prince! How could our army possibly take on an army of countless millions? Much less mount an offensive push into enemy territory." Zeto sat down to the agreement of many around him.

"We have just crushed the southern army. It will take

time for Bazetar to make another, and it will take time for the forces to the north or the west to return to the Castillo Morta. We have a few weeks to prepare. Once we take the outer wall we can hold off the Trowcan army while our divine lords handle the Troll King." The leadership erupted in chatter. Nwendor simply sat there watching them all argue. He looked down at his hands still showing sign of blood in the fold and wrinkles. It reminded him of the massacre he committed years earlier.

"What do the divine say?" the voice of Zeto disrupted his train of thought and the room quieted.

"Matiun, your tactics helped win us this day. The Trowcans were soundly defeated. Do you think our forces could carry out the Sagen prince's plan?" Nwendor's eyes fixed on Matiun, who stood while adjusting his circular lensed glasses.

"Lords, we are hopelessly outnumbered. We are logistically ill equipped. Still we are battle hardened, and have the resolve needed to succeed. We will need to seek help from others who are still able to muster forces."

"Who? Who is still around?" asked Migus.

"There are the giants of Koglan to the Northwest. Last we heard the Trowcans could not penetrate their defenses. There are also the people of Diablo Surr." The council erupted in disagreement on the subject of the Diablo and Diablo Surriens were well known savage raiders.

"I know it sounds ridiculous but we could use their savagery to our advantage. All we need is to get messengers over to their islands." Matiun look around at the faces that all seemed to fold at the idea of sending emissaries to the other side of the continent.

"I'll go!" shouted Nyka with her hand raised.

"No you most certainly will not." Said Nwendor as Nyka

sat back down waiting for the opportunity to discuss the matter with her father privately.

"Diablo Surr is an Island that is very volcanically active, not to mention the violent locals. Even if we send messengers there at this instant, they will never reach them in time." Zeto pleaded to Matiun.

"We would be glad to lend our assistance." A voice poked through the open doors of the balcony. A tall, slender pale skinned man hovered into the space his feet dragging on the floor.

"Good evening gentlemen. We are the..."

"We know who you are foul creature." Said Marcus.

"You are the Vampire of Montania. We are divine, and can see right through your trickery." The council still and quiet looked puzzled.

"Eww, gross how their skin just hangs like that." Exclaimed Migus while he put his hand over his mouth. The vampires of Montania were known as the dark seducers. Their ability to make their grotesque appearance look irresistible to either male of female secured many victims. The gods were able to see past the illusion to their true form. They had huge black eyes, no nose, and a mouth full of needle like teeth used to pierce skin. Their legs were half the length of their long clawed arms and their skin looked like raw chicken skin left out in the sun. Upon hearing that they were exposed, they began to back away slightly.

"My lords please, we are not here to hurt anyone. We simply want to help you defeat the Trowcan menace before they wipe us all out. I am Ilget and this is Atoode. We were present when King Crenon prevailed all those years ago, but this time the stakes are much higher. We can fly to Diablo Surr and deliver your message in a few days instead of weeks." Ilget pleaded.

“What difference does it make to your revolting kind whether we live or not? Why don’t you just feed on the Trowcans?” asked Migus.

“They are a race that should have never existed. They poison the very ground they tread and the water they drink. We cannot feed on them because their blood is toxic to us.”

“I see, so they are killing off you food supply. Pretty soon you’ll all starve.” Migus laughed.

“They can’t be trusted.” Whispered Migus to Marcus and Nwendor.

“If we do not send them then we’ll definitely be short an ally.” Said Marcus. Nwendor left the whispering huddle and sat upright giving the plan some thought.

“Vampire lords of the north. We will accept your help, on the condition you leave our people alone. There will be absolutely no feeding here.” The two vampires bowed to Nwendor as he stood from his seat and signaled Matiun over.

“We will need to send a messenger to speak to the giants as well. Come with me Matiun. We have work to do. Vampires, see yourselves out.” Nwendor and Matiun left the room as Marcus walked over to the vampires and gave them a scroll of paper to deliver. They slowly crept out of the palace window, and flew into the starry night sky. The illusion of safety withered from the mortal council and was replaced with a feeling of dread.

“Out of the question!” Nwendor’s voice echoed through the palace.

“I am not a child anymore father! I am 19 and fully capable of this mission.”

“I forbid it! You will stay here while I am away. Do you hear me!” Nwendor smashed his fist on the table sending splinters in all directions.

"Let her go Lord Nwendor, she has more than proven her worth in battle."

"Migus! How did you get past my guards?" asked Nwendor as Migus as he strolled casually into the room leaning his spear on the broken table.

"Please, those puny mortals make it way too easy."

"I will remedy that, but for now I am having a discussion with my daughter, so I will have to ask you to leave."

"I am part of this planning committee..."

"War council!" Nwendor corrected.

"Fine. War council." Migus wiggled his fingers at Nwendor, mocking him.

"Lord Migus is right! I should be able to go without your permission." Nyka stood firm, balling her fists and glared at her father.

"Well I am only here to be a part of the process. Will we be get medals or badges?"

"Shut up!" Nwendor said to the indifferent Migus.

"Nyka, my love, I..."

"She is the only other divine being here. So, she will either use her super abilities to combat the Troll King, or take a leisurely stroll to the giant's realm to give them a message. Which sounds more dangerous to you?" Nwendor stayed silent with Nyka's eyes fixed on his face waiting for a reaction. Migus stretched out on a long padded bench with his hands behind his head exhaling in satisfaction.

"Father, I am highly skilled and highly trained. I can do this." She held her fists to her chest while walking closer to her father.

“Don’t forget tenacious. Just like your Dad.” Migus interjected.

“There is no better person for the task.” She pleaded with her father holding his palms and looking into his eyes. He saw Irlan glancing back at him through her and his heart melted.

“Okay I will allow you to go once we arrive at the port of Kreshant and you will be taking an escort with you. That is non-negotiable. Do you understand?” he said as he pointed at her.

“Yes father!” she jumped up and hugged Nwendor around his neck with both arms. He began to leave the room to go find a group of soldiers to accompany her.

“They grow so fast.” Migus stood there with his arm outstretched waiting for a hug from Nwendor.

“If you ever interfere in my private affairs again and we will have to revisit the central arena.” Nwendor walked away leaving Migus still waiting for a hug.

“I guess I’ll just see myself out like the Vampires.” He stood on a balcony and performed a series of flips and high jumps till he was at his own palace.

6

"It is time for lunch my students. Please make your way over to the table in an orderly fashion." Stosay held his arm out pointing the students in the direction of the dining table. Stosay placed bowls in front of the kids and filled them with a hot meaty stew he had been cooking over the fireplace. After everyone was served he gave them permission to eat. The children greedily ate the delicious soup which had all manner of vegetables along with tender pieces of oily meat.

"Master Stosay I must say this stew is excellent." said Crux while taking in another spoon full. The other children agreed that the meal was tasty and continued to fill their bellies.

"It is too bad Beth is not here to try this. I think she would have loved it." said Maya.

"Oh my girl, do not worry about little Bethany. I almost feel like she is with all of us right now." Stosay began to chuckle, softly at first but then erupted into full blown maniacal laughter. The children looked at each other, wondering why that was so funny to their teacher. The candles in the school began to pulse lightly and then stopped when his laughter died down.

"Eat my children you do not want B… ugh, the soup, to get cold." He giggled.

"Eat every last drop." His voice deepened as he remained perfectly still.

"Listen as I begin the next chapter."

A Fleet Of Hope

Nwendor stood on the bow of a Sagen ship. The sound of the ocean along with the cool sea breeze soothed him. He closed his eyes and saw Irlan as he always did. She was smiling at him and moved her lips to quietly say, “I love you”. For a fleeting moment he felt her warmth when suddenly the sound of footsteps running to the edge of the ship snapped him out of his daydream. It was Zeto vomiting chunks of his lunch into the ocean. The Yagan leader had never been off his island even on a ship before.

“I’m sorry lord, I couldn’t help it.”

“It’s quite alright Zeto. How are the rest of the Yagan troops faring?”

“Not good at all my lord. They are all seasick.” Zeto hung his head over the rail and let loose again. Nwendor patted his back and walked up to the helmsman followed by Pykas. He nodded to the young man and proceeded to the aft deck. There he took in the view of the entire fleet. It was massive with ship sails lining the horizon like clouds. As he admired the spectacular view Pykas growled at the footsteps approaching them.

“What is it boy?” asked Nwendor while stroking the hound’s neck fur.

“Impressive isn’t it?” asked Matiun

“Very. How is all this even possible? The logistics alone.”

“The fleet is strong and full of men and women alike who have lost a lot in this war. Their determination and resolve keep this machine sailing.”

"Suppose we get attacked at sea? How will the ship protect themselves?"

"The gods made Boe Chantra a land that rapidly evolves warfare. When we fought Bazetar the first time we had catapults and trebuchets. Now we have something new that had been spreading on the continent. Let me show you. This way." Nwendor ordered Pykas to stay above decks making the Battle Hound whine and whimper as the two men went below to the first gun deck.

"These are cannon. All our ships carry at least 15 on each side. The great Aires, your father, has blessed us with this new technology. Only the biggest fool would ever try to attack us." Nwendor thought of his father. He hadn't seen him in year and knew the war god would be very pleased at the sight of these cannon. As long as war continued and mortals still worshipped him, he would keep his power. They had been at sail for a long time and would arrive at Kreshant the following day. Marcus and Migus were each on separate ships. Marcus had said goodbye to his family whom he was extremely secretive about. Migus packed luxury items to make the trip feel more like a cruise than a military operation.

On another ship sat Nyka on a barrel of ale while sharpening her sword with a stone. Dotoria was back to her original size and was sleeping at her feet. Nyka felt the blade edge and shaved off a very thin flake of skin that didn't bleed. After sheathing the sword she pulled out her throwing knives and began to sharpen them also. Dotoria opened her eyes, lifted her head sharply and began to growl. Altor walked over to Nyka and stood next to her.

"Easy girl." Nyka said

"You should put that thing in a cage below deck." Altor pointed at Dotoria who promptly snapped at his finger missing by an inch.

"Really Nyka, that thing is dangerous and ugly."

"I think she's just the cutest little dragon ever." Nyka grabbed Dotoria's head with both hands and lightly shook it side to side. The dragon's tongue hung out of its mouth which almost resembled a smile.

"What brings you here Altor?"

"Well I am pleased to tell you that I requested, and got approved to join you on your little quest."

"What? Altor it will be far too dangerous for you. You've never seen action anywhere."

"Yes, that is true but I feel I must be there to protect my future wife."

"What? Altor we are not even engaged yet. How can you say that? I really believe that you should..." Altor quickly knelt at Nyka's feet presenting a gold ring with a pink diamond on top. Nyka's eyes widened in horror as he grabbed on to her hand.

"My Princess Nyka, would you do me the honor of being my wife?" he grabbed her ring finger gently and began to slide the ring on. Nyka was at a loss for words for the first time in her life. Before she knew it, the ring was all the way to the base of her finger. Nyka stood in shock as Altor grabbed both her hands in his while smiling at her. He leaned in to give her a quick peck on the lips and clapped his hands in excitement. I will go make all the necessary arrangements. He walked off towards the entrance to the lower decks where two of his friends asked him how it went as they disappeared into the ship.

"What just happened?" Nyka gestured to Dotoria who just tilted her head in confusion.

Nwendor continued his walk around the gun deck marveling at the iron tubes aimed at the ocean.

"Lord Nwendor, I have been meaning to give you this. It is a message that was stuck to my cabin door with a knife." Matiun handed a paper with dried blood keeping it sealed. He opened the note knowing exactly what it was and who it was from.

"We are coming for you" the note said.

"My lord if I may ask."

"No! No, you may not." Nwendor crumbled up the paper and threw it to the bulkhead where it bounced off and rested on the deck. He stormed off leaving Matiun speechless. He did not dare pick up the paper and went about his duties instead.

On Abel's ship he sat on the rails surrounded by his guard discussing tactics and preparation for the landing. As they laughed at an inappropriate comment made by one of the men, a little boy clad in armor showed up and sat on a crate. His feet were suspended in the air 6 inches shy of touching the floor.

"Xenon, what are you doing here?"

"I am the king and I want to be informed of everything." The little boy crossed his arms.

"Little brother, these matters pertain to adults, are the nurses not..."

"I apologize my lord, but the little king insisted." said Greta his old nurse. Able looked to both and took a deep breath.

"Very well, Xenon we are talking about securing our landing at the port of Kreshant and advancing into the city, eventually reaching the castle." He continued discussing the plan as the boy king slumped on the crate more and more as the planning continued. He rested his head on his hands and let out various yawns before the 8 year old lost interest and left to play in his cabin. Abel dismissed his guard soon after and leaned on the rail. Though he was all business when it came to his country, he couldn't shake his feelings for Nyka. He looked at her ship as it rocked on the water and wondered what she was doing. At that moment 2 men approached him from behind.

"Well, well, well. Look what we have here, an unescorted prince. What should we do with him Billy?" the man looked to his partner. Abel turned around still leaning on the rail with his elbows.

"What can I do for you gentlemen?" asked Abel.

"Look you, I know you're a Sagen prince but that doesn't mean anything to us." Billy put his finger in Abel's face as he spoke.

"We are only going to tell you one time. Leave the princess Nyka alone. She is spoken for." Abel smiled at the men making them feel insulted from his lack of fear.

"Oh, I see how it's going to be." Both men balled their fists and began walking closer to the prince. Suddenly they were thrown on the ground and had swords at their necks. Abel had seen members of his guard approach the two thugs silently.

"Please my lord, we weren't going to harm you"

"We were just going to rough you up a bit." Billy said.

"No we were not. Shut up!" the leader of the two tried to slap Billy but was restrained by the guardsmen.

"Right. Who sent you?" Abel now stood with his hands on his hips.

"You'll never get it out of us right Billy?"

"Yeah! Master Altor paid us more than enough for our silence." Billy's eyes widened and both men bowed their heads in defeat. The other thug managed to give Billy a kick in the seat of his pants.

"Okay, I think we've gotten all the useful information

these two have to offer. Off to the brig with you two." The men were hauled off as the leader of the guard started giving orders.

"Captain, send the men to their berthing. I'll be fine. We've got a big day tomorrow and they need to be rested." The captain did not feel at ease leaving hid prince unprotected but followed orders and Abel was left alone again with his thoughts.

The following day the ship bustled with activity. All the soldiers were armed and armored, the cannons were loaded and ready to fire. Kreshant was now in sight with plumes of smoke rising at various points. The sky was completely gray with thick clouds blocking the sun. The Castillo Morta stood out not because of its magnificent size, the countless towers reaching to the sky, or even the fact that it was built on a mountain top surrounded by a crater. The upper section of the castle had an orb shield surrounding it. It was a last ditch effort of the gods to hold in Bazetar. The orb looked like a clear glass sphere except for the occasional crackle of light and electricity that could be heard for miles. Once the ships made it into the harbor there was commotion ashore. They saw Trowcans trying to set up a defense to repel them. Normally this would have been handled by the southern army but since its destruction, these were all Bazetar could muster. The forward most ships turned broadside and began pulverizing the landing zone with cannon fire. Volley after volley peppered the coast as hundreds of small boats rowed ashore. Arrows began landing in the water around them and Marcus and Migus responded with fire and lightning attacks. No one was lost in the landing as the combined Yagan and Sagen army began taking the streets. The few Trowcans still there were slaughtered quickly. Their usual tactic was overwhelming numbers, but in this small a group and with minimal light armor, they were easy pickings.

The army continued till noon securing the city and gathering supplies. Abel ordered them to take as much food and water as they could. The rations were stored for the meantime in preparation for the assault on the castle. If the causeway was still there they would be able to reach the gate before nightfall. Resistance intensified as the army walked up the path to rim of the crater and the entrance to the causeway. Arrows attacked their metal shields but had no impact on the armored column of men marching down the causeway to the gate. The causeway was 20ft wide and half a mile long and stood 750ft at its deepest point within the crater. It was held up by massive stone pillars spaced out every hundred feet. The floor was adorned with mosaic pieces showing the history of the gods and Kreshant. Once the column reached the gate plaza, they had a wall to either side of them, and the gatehouse in front. The soldiers were greeted by all sorts of projectile being cast down from the main walls. The mass of men filled the plaza, creating a conveyer belt passing ladders forward. Once they were raised to the top, the treacherous climb began. Nwendor appeared from under his kite shield and extended his claws. He stabbed the stones of the castle wall penetrating it allowing him to climb with great speed like a gecko. Marcus and Migus fired on the archers posted above. Once at the top of the wall, Nwendor went into another frenzy, killing the Trowcan defenders around the ladders. Once the men made it to the top he changed his focus over to the gatehouse. He killed the 10 defenders and began turning the wheel raising the metal portcullis. Hundreds of soldiers poured into the castle wiping out the Trowcans on the main wall and beyond. They were instructed not to venture close to the orb shield because Bazetar could be lying in wait on the other side. The sun began to set and their quick victory was celebrated among the ranks of men. The Sagen army was finally home. The men were not allowed to visit their homes until the danger was over.

From the Eagle's lookout the Troll King stared at the intruders at his doorstep. This was most unfortunate. He knew he could take the entire army on by himself, but the fact that there was not 1, but 3 lesser gods against him made him worry. He remembered them vaguely as he always thought the lesser gods inferior, and not worth his time. Now they were here with a formidable force poised to destroy his plans for the world. He sighed and returned to the throne room where he saw Sadanasia watching two Trowcans battle to the death. She clapped in fulfilled entertainment as one disemboweled the other. She heard Bazetar take his seat next to her and she gestured for the surviving Trowcan to leave.

"Hello my king, any news from the garrison?"

"The garrison has been wiped out!" he answered in annoyance.

"Oh, but you can make more. It is just a small inconvenience."

"Is this all you've been doing?"

"You sound like my parents. Is moping about the castle all you've been doing? You should be making more Trowcans for when we destroy the orb shield."

"You do not command me!" growled Bazetar pounding his armrest.

"I am leaving now. This is something the king has to deal with, not his beautiful queen." She stood and strutted out of the throne room, her hips swaying from side to side in an exaggerated fashion. Bazetar growled furiously at the ever spoiled queen. He sat there wondering how he was going to destroy the mortals and why his queen seemed indifferent to their plight. He began to wander aimlessly from corridor to corridor in the almost empty castle. Only a handful of Trowcans were left and were under strict orders not to engage the humans for they could not be spared. Their job now was to wait on the king and queen. He walked past a room Sadanasia visited every few weeks or so. He heard an angelic voice singing a tune from the Kreshant culture. It was a happy song about lovers meeting and raising little ones to honor the gods. He pressed his pointed ear to the door and lost himself in the tranquility of Sarre's voice. When the song was over he slowly opened the door.

"What do you want now Sada..." she let out a shriek and covered herself with her blanket as if it would protect her from the god of the dead.

"Why did you stop singing?" he said in a deep voice. Sarre was now shivering and hyperventilating. Her wide open eyes studied the giant figure standing in the doorway.

"Perhaps this will help." A cool blue mist left his 3 fingered claw and drifted over to Sarre who held her breath and shut her eyes. She let out a sigh of relief as the mist soothed her skin and her insides, even reaching her mind putting her at ease.

"What was that?" she asked opening her eyes slowly.

"Mist of the Ellowes. Not all my power is based on the dark practices. It is meant to heal. Though I am Bazetar, you have no reason to fear me at the moment. Now, answer the question. Why did you stop singing?"

"I reached the end of the song and don't know many others."

"I will appoint you as the royal serenader. You will be stationed in my throne room and will sing to me when I wish it. Understood?" Sarre looked down to his wide clawed feet. This was the being that killed her parents and destroyed her country, yet he had been the only one to treat her like a human being in recent times.

"Your reply?" he said calmly but with a bit of agitation.

"I will humbly serve you King of the Trowcans." She said in a soft trembling voice.

"Wrong girl. I am the king of all." He sent a black beam

from his fingertip that hit her chains and made the links crumble into dust.

"Your queen will be furious when she sees me wandering about."

"The matter is noted but her feelings are not at all my concern. I expect you to find something suitable to wear. Those rags will not do." He held his hands behind his back and his heavy steps echoed through the halls as he walked farther away. Sarre was started to cry. She hated the feeling of being in the service of that monster, but she had no choice. She walked to her old room that was completely untouched and changed into one of her favorite dresses. A Trowcan minder was sent to always keep tabs on her. The Trowcan known as Gara, followed her everywhere she went and taunted her along the way. Though she was not in a favorable position in life she did give it her all. Almost anything was better than being chained to the floor all day. She went to the library and learned different songs which she practiced in her room. Her look and sound intrigued the Troll King. He did not know what he was feeling but he knew that he felt more at ease every time she was around.

The invaders had secured the entire lower castle and the city. To the amazement of the armies there were some survivors of the Trowcan invasion. Many had hidden in bunkers obscured from view and the few began to make their way to the castle. Many chambers were converted into stockpiles for supplies and provisions. Matiun again was put in charge of the castle defenses. He ordered the surviving civilians to be placed in the soft vaults to weather the coming siege. The soft vaults were simply reenforced concrete and stone rooms with a large iron door that could only be unlocked from the inside. The old man tirelessly tended to the defenses. He ordered barrels of gun powder be placed at the base of the columns supporting the causeway. He wondered if the Trowcans would even be able to reach the walls if it was destroyed. The chasm surrounding the castle was immensely deep and wide. They were in a very strong defensible position.

Nwendor stood at the main gate viewing with the portcullis overhead. He waited for his little girl who he knew was not little anymore to arrive. He still saw the face of the infant Irlan held somewhere in there. Nyka's men passed on horseback, bowing their heads in respect. They were members of the acclaimed Sagen cavalry. Nyka rode out mounted on Pykas who whined wanting to keep up with the horses passing him. She jumped off the battle hound and walked to her father.

"A fine animal you have there." She turned to glance at Pykas and then back to face her father.

"He is as loyal as he is ferocious." Dotoria flew past them and continued across the causeway. Nwendor's eyes followed the gift from his father to his daughter.

"How is... the little dragon working out for you?"

"Dotoria? She is great. She follows me everywhere I go."

"I am glad you got to meet your grandfather. He is a great and just god. Far more righteous than I." Nwendor's face became serious as he stared into his daughter's eyes.

"I know I can't convince you to abandon this endeavor but I will ask one more time regardless."

"Father, there is no need to worry or even send a crew to help me. This mission will succeed." Nwendor tilted his head, put his hands on her shoulders, and pulled her in for a hug. She sniffled a bit and raised her hand to wipe her nose.

"A ring?" he grabbed her hand with a lightning-fast movement and inspected it.

"Did Altor propose marriage?" he raised one eyebrow.

"Father I am not so..."

"Ah my great future father in law. I see you have been made aware of the upcoming nuptials. I am pleased to grace your family with my family's last name." his horse continued to walk down the causeway as Altor continued talking not even bowing his head to Nwendor as he strode by.

"You don't seem too sure Nyka. Are you having doubts?"

"Since he put the damned thing on my finger." Her father's face soured and he released her hand.

"Then you need to tell him that you are not ready and if he doesn't listen to reason, you let me know."

"I'll be fine father. I can handle myself. I have to go." She hugged her father tightly, released him running over to Pykas and speeding over to the knights sworn to protect her. They rode off and disappeared behind the edge of crater's rim. From a tower watched Abel, through an old cracked telescope he found buried under debris he had kicked up with his foot.

A great distance away from the action at Kreshant was the Trowcan Northern Army. It was laying siege to the gate that led into the country of Koglan, the land of the giants. The gate towered 100ft in height and had cliffs that stood 50ft higher than it on both sides. The Trowcans used trebuchets to pound the reinforced double doors but stones had no effect on the iron sheets protecting them. Still they were urged to continue by their general, the indifferent Kragnus. He sat at his chair with his upper lip permanently raised on one side showing his sharp teeth.

"General, the King wishes to speak to you." A soldier said. Kragnus got out of his chair very slowly, letting out a big yawn and stretching his arms out. He began walking slowly over to a beacon the size of an ale barrel. There its black center crystal began to glow and a deep rumbling voice emanated from it.

"Listen now, your king speaks" Bazetar's voice filled the

tent.

“Are all my generals there?”

“Colled, general of the western army, at your service my king.”

“Setasan, general of the mountain army, at your service my king.”

“...Kragnus, high general of the Northern army, still stuck here in Kolgan, at your service my king.”

“Forred and the southern army have been completely annihilated by the army of Tridom.” The generals’ eyes widened at the news except for Kragnus. He just scowled at the black crystal hoping someone was able to see his expression.

“They are here besieging the Castillo Morta. All forces are recalled back to Kreshant. We will destroy the mortals and then invade Tridom. Once the country is conquered we will resume the conquest of Boe Chantra.”

“My lord, there is no need to bring all the armies home. Kragnus is the closest and his army has been stalled at the giant’s doorstep long enough. He has more than enough troops to get the job done. Only a fool would fail. Let us maintain our grip here in the west, and the northern mountains so as not to give these sheep a chance to regroup.” Setasan continued to plead his case to Bazetar who listened silently. Though he was the supreme authority, he was not against listening to sound advice. The lord of the Trowcans relented and allowed them to stay in their current positions. Only Kragnus and the northern army would return to retake the castle. The other two generals signed off and returned to their work. Kragnus was furious though he hid it well from Bazetar.

“There is another matter Kragnus. The human Matiun must be dealt with. I do not wish for out army to get torn apart again by his siege defenses. Give your army their marching orders and start heading this way on your own. You will be alone and covert in this mission. That will be all." The beacon dimmed into a black rock, Kragnus began throwing things and knocking furniture over. How dare Colled and Setasan suggest that he be the one to break his siege. He was the top commander of the Trowcans the first time they invaded, way before these two were even born, died, and resurrected from the Plains of Sorrow. Kragnus stormed out of the tent and shouted a command to all.

"Prepare the army! We're leaving!" he ordered his captains to march the army to Kreshant where he would meet up with them once they arrived. The siege of Koglan was lifted and the giants could be heard cheering the departure of the Trowcans from the safety of their walls.

7

"That will be all for today my students. Please go in an orderly fashion to the front door." The students lined up and began to chat and bicker for a bit. They quickly remembered the terrible aura emitted from their teacher and settled down. Parents were waiting outside in the cold for their children. Stosay opened the door, and the kids ran out in the snow. Some parents showed their delight while embracing their children while other were colder towards them.

"Master Stosay, how are you sir?" Mr. Tolber, father of Wren asked trying to get Stosay's attention.

"How are you my good sir? I hope that the children are behaving well." He asked again.

"Well you know chil…"

"Excellent, excellent. Did you hear about the Helts?" Mr. Tolber wrestled with Wren trying to keep him still.

"…No… I did not. Why don't you tell me?" darkness enveloped Stosay's surroundings making everyone outside stop in their tracks.

"Well it turns out that the entire household was murdered last night." The darkness lifted and Stosay became cheery again.

"You don't say? What a terrible occurrence. And little Beth?" he asked with feigned curiosity, leaning closer to Mr. Tolber.

"All of them were torn apart by some vicious animal. There were claw and teeth marks everywhere. Little Bethany was not spared. The monster pounded on her head till only mush was left and a sizable chunk of her anatomy was missing." Stosay's mittened hand rose to cover his mask's smiling mouth.

"You just never know what will happen. Good day to you Mr. Tolber. I must be off." Stosay locked the door to the school and walked away quickly.

Rise Of The 5

Nyka and her band rode across a great distance stopping only at night to rest. Sadly the land was barren, void of life. All the animals and people had already been consumed. The journey took them through Bole Va and the western edge of the East Shore before reaching Koglan. No danger was encountered due to the Trowcans moving like a wildfire, leaving few if any behind. As they rode a gray cloud loomed on the horizon. The northern army was on the move south towards Kreshant. Quickly Nyka and her men hid by a rocky outcrop at the top of a hill.

"That is going to be a huge problem." Captain Rossen said as he viewed the river of soldiers marching

"Yes, it appears so." Nyka whispered under her breath.

"Have you ever seen anything like this before?" asked another soldier. They were in a column formation and the head nor the rear could be seen. The Trowcans stared forward to the south, not even caring about the scenery around them. It almost looked like they were in a kind of trance.

"We need to get out of here. The horses will give away our position."

"I agree Rossen, let's go." Nyka signaled to the men. The group crept to their mounts and rode off before they could be spotted. They continued riding north to where the gray clouds disappeared behind them. As the sun began to set, they stopped and rested next to a bubbling creek. Pykas emerged from the trees with a lone deer that had escaped the Trowcans in his mouth. Dotoria landed next to him and tried to snap at the lifeless deer. Pykas growled and jumped away from her greedily trying to enjoy his catch alone. Nyka told him to release the carcass which bounced on the ground. With her thin sword she sliced off a hind leg and threw it to Dotoria who flew to a high perch and began eating her meal. Pykas grabbed the rest and began ripping it apart.

"That is disgusting." Rossen turned away as the animal's guts fell all over the ground.

"How are you feeling princess?"

"I am anxious to meet the giants. I feel having them as an ally will help us win."

"No one alive even knows what they even look like. Except maybe you father and his kin but not us. Those gates have been closed for a very long time. Not since the times of the Rowads have they emerged."

"Rowads? Who or what were they?" Rossen sat near the fire resting his sword at his feet.

"The Rowads were a band of savages that brought the continent to its knees around 600 years ago. They pillaged and destroyed many countries setting them back many years. The Rowads were not human, they were covered in scales and had a long slender frame. They stood at least 7 feet tall and were extremely adept fighters. Only a sole army was able to muster against them and even the giants were convinced to help. During the battle of North Laguna, they were finally defeated, and the land was saved. Afterwards the giants returned to their country and built the iron gate to keep all out. They had had enough war and did not want to mess in the affairs of the different nations ever again."

"I see. I wonder how we're going to get in there. If the Trowcans weren't able to do it, how will we?"

"Only time will tell princess." Rossen laid back resting his head on his folded cape and rolled to his side. He was asleep in seconds. Nyka rested her arms on her folded knees staring into the small campfire.

"How are you my dear?" Nyka cringed at the voice of Altor just as her mother would to Norques.

"It seems we are quite alone at the moment." Altor motioned to the sleeping group of men and shot her a provocative grin. She reached for her blanket hoping he would understand that she needed to get some rest. His face went from a smile to an angry frown. Nyka noticed this and quickly looked to her ring finger. She had forgotten to put the ring back on her finger. Nyka had removed it because she did not feel comfortable wearing it. She kicked herself mentally for being so absent minded. She tried to keep Altor at distance the entire journey, always giving an excuse as to why she could not be bothered. Her plan was to keep him believing the wedding was going to happen until they returned, and let him down gently after the battle if they somehow survived.

"Where is the ring? Don't tell me you lost it?"

"I have it right here in my pocket." She reached in with her narrow fingers and pulled out the ring.

"As my fiancée I expect you to always have that ring on your finger regardless of what is going on at the moment. Put it on now." He demanded waking the sleeping soldiers at his feet. He held his position with a finger still pointing at Nyka's hand.

"Alright this has gone on for long enough. Altor I am not a woman to be controlled by any man. Let alone one I can obliterate with one hand. I felt sorry for leading you on, but now that I see your true nature, nothing makes me happier than to declare what little we were before is now over. I am the commanding officer of this detail and I expect you to follow my orders no question." She threw the ring at Altor as the soldiers on the ground listened, pretending to be asleep. Altor was speechless and just stood there with the ring in his hand. Nyka bid him good night and laid on her side for some much needed sleep. Eventually Altor left his daze and walked out of view to where his belongings were. The fire continued crackling into the cool night air.

The following morning the order was given to mount up. All the soldiers listened without question, including Altor who had not spoken a word. They rode for hours following the long trail left by the Trowcans. The tales of the giant gate did not do it any justice. It had to be seen with the naked eye to appreciate its gargantuan size. They all marveled at it until Nyka snapped everyone out of it and commanded them to dawn climbing gear. 3 men including Altor who wasn't much of a climber stayed to protect the horses and Pykas below, while Nyka and 4 others began to scale the cliff wall. After about 20 minutes of slow climbing with a break in the middle they reached the top. Dotoria simply flew and waited for them to arrive. Nyka told them to remain where they were because she did not know if the giants were still manning the wall. She pulled herself up and crouched listening for any type of movement. Dotoria panted and scratched herself on the cliff wall that was over 60ft thick and made of solid rock. She walked to the edge where the gates were positioned 50ft below her.

"No one is here." She whispered loud enough so the men could hear her. They all got to the top and ran over to her. On the other side was Koglan, a land not seen by non-citizens for centuries.

"We'll head for that location. I do believe that is where they'll be." Nyka said while pointing to the group of very tall stone structures. They dropped ropes and began their descent to the other side. Dotoria flew to the base of the gate and waited.

Altor was lost in thought, staring into the distance. He

was not focused on anything but the thought of being rejected. He excused himself from the other 2 men saying he had to relieve himself. The men told him to be quick. Altor walked through trees and abandoned siege works. He found a place where he would not be visible to the other men or Pykas and sat down. Slowly a tear began to roll down his face. He felt genuinely bad for how he treated Nyka. He always just assumed that that was the way all women were to be treated. That was how his mother had been treated and she never once complained. At that moment a shadowy figure put a hand over his mouth and took him. Not a sound was made.

Nyka signaled her men to stop and get low to the ground. Thunderous footsteps approached their position. The giant was right on top of them in one step and far away the next, oblivious to them even being there. It looked to be about 60ft tall, wearing trousers and boots made from an unknown hide. The muscular giant was also shirtless and covered in tattoos on only its left side. The thing continued on its path as the humans made their way over to a gathering of vertical stone slabs arranged into a circle. Once there the humans snuck around the many giants engaged in a celebration of sorts. A bonfire blazed in the center made up of numerous dry trunks of whole pine trees. The giants ate the meat off a carcass almost 3 times their own size. Its legs pointed to the sky as steaks that were enough to feed an army were carved. The food was served on plates made of iron and the size of ponds. The giants conversed, danced, and behaved as any other person would only in different proportions. One Giant sat on a massive boulder chiseled into the form of a seat. He wore a gold crown that wrapped around his hairless head and could be used to pen cattle. All the male giants were bald and the women had a small area on the back of their head where hair a single tuft of hair grew. The hair was long and was braided into lengths of 30ft or more. The giant in the center raised his hand and everyone became quiet.

"For many centuries we have preserved our way of life." The crowd murmured in agreement.

"The little gray invaders thought they could come here and claim what is not theirs." The crowd grew louder.

"If the tiny grays or men try to come here we will give them all a good stomping. They are no match for us, we are giants and tower above all!" he raised his fist to the heavens as the giants cheered in jubilation. He gave a gesture to settle down.

"We are solid like our walls, I ask you now. Is there anyone that can stop us?"

"Yes there is!" yelled Nyka as she walked out onto the floor of the celebration.

"An intruder!" yelled a giant female picking her child off the floor. There was a lot of commotion that was calmed down by the surprised leader as he walked over to the tiny Nyka.

"It is a tiny man! How did you get past our walls?" he got on all fours and examined her with his left eye which was the size of a cow.

"I am Nyka, daughter of King Nwendor, son of Aires." The giant stood and let out a hearty laugh.

"You are the granddaughter of a true god? Do you have any proof?" he continued chuckling with his hands resting on his belly. She looked to her left and let out a sharp whistle. Out flew Dotoria from the vegetation where she had been hiding and landed next to her.

"I have a dragon that was given to me by my grandfather. Her name is Dotoria." Some oohs and ahs were heard but the leader was still not convinced.

"So you have an exotic pet. That means nothing. Koglan is full of creatures even more peculiar than that spotted dragon."

He pointed at the growling Dotoria.

"Okay, well what if she shows you, my grandfather. Would you believe me then?" the giants all nodded to each other in agreement.

"Show them what you can do..." she walked away from Dotoria who pointed her muzzle upwards and shot out purple flames that contorted as it rose above the heads of the giants. A figure began forming and then took the shape of Aires.

"Great giants of Koglan, I am Aires, the war god. I hear you do not take my granddaughter's word as valid and truthful. Is this so?" the deep voice unsettled the giants making some of them faint making minor earthquakes when they crashed into the ground.

"King Doschen. Do you feel my Nyka is a liar?" Aires's armored head came so close to Doschen that his eyes crossed as he trembled with fear. He shook his head nervously communicating no to the war god. Aires's effigy stood erect still looking down on the giants.

"I applaud the victory you have won here, it will be recorded in the annals of our hall of records. I bid you farewell giants" the fire vanished and Dotoria snapped out of the trance-like state she was in. She looked to Nyka with her tongue hanging out. Nyka looked around at the scared giants. She raised her arms to them.

"Great giants, we have come to ask that you join us in finishing off the Trowcans. As we speak the army that was just at your gates marches south to the Castillo Morta. There Bazetar is trapped but the Orb Shield will not hold him for long. That is why the gods are helping us. His war affects us all, and will leave chaos and devastation everywhere, even here. Yes, you all are huge and strong, but the Troll King possesses powerful sorcery that will undo you with ease. Join us." The crowd discussed amongst themselves and a couple of older giants whispered in Doschen's ear. He turned and raised his hands to the crowd.

"We have maintained a policy of isolationism for many years now. If we go and leave our lands to assist you it will not be a light decision. We as a people must vote on this and it will take time regardless of your lineage."

"I think you all are being cowards!" shouted Rossen in frustration. Nyka shot him an angry look and turned back to the giant King.

"Please forgive my compatriot. We have been in a constant state of battle for..."

"Nyka of the tiny people. We the giants will go over this matter and will show up if we so choose. Give us our privacy as we contemplate our decision. We ask that you all leave immediately. Have a good night." He motioned to two giants who came close and gestured towards the gate. Many giants whined that the celebration was ruined.

"Goodbye giants." Said Nyka turning around and leaving. They were escorted to the gate and allowed to exit before the gate slammed shut with extreme force that made the ground shake.

"What a disaster. Rossen you are a soldier not a politician. Next time keep your mouth shut." They began to walk to the area where they left the horses. They were all there with Pykas but the 3 men were gone. They called to the them with no answer. Nyka mounted Pykas and the other men their horses as they began to search around the trees and siege engines that littered the area. Out of nowhere appeared Altor holding a wound on his head where it appeared something had struck him.

"What happened? Where are the other 2?"

"Nyka is that you. I was attacked by Trowcans. They came

out of the brush; I was barely able to escape but the others are still with them. I think they're going to eat them.

"Where? Where are they?" shouted Nyka.

"Over there by those trees." He said weakly before collapsing to the ground. The remaining detail galloped over to the trees with their blades drawn. As Nyka approached, she was knocked clean off of Pykas and she hit the ground. She had never been hit that hard in her life. She held her nose and stood holding out her sword.

"Princess! Are you..." something quick, left a trail of red and silver passing right through the soldier and his horse. They both fell to the ground in two pieces. Pykas was captured in a huge metal net by something moving too fast for him to register in time to react. Nyka saw the black hooded person but did not know who it was. She ran over to try to free Pykas but was attacked again by two hooded figures that moved just as fast and were as strong as she was. She tried to parry their moves, but they were too many. She managed to grab one of her throwing knives and fling it to one of the moving shadows. It let out a scream while holding its leg and tumbling on the ground. At that moment Dotoria shot her purple fire into the trees lighting them up to where the shadow people were easier to see. One shadow stood atop Pykas now laying on his side.

"That is enough!" he held a spear aimed between Pykas's ribs.

"No stop! Don't hurt him!" Nyka pleaded.

"Drop your weapons. Now!" she, Rossen, and 2 of the remaining soldiers dropped their arms.

"What do you want?" she asked.

"Tell your lizard to come down here." She whistled for Dotoria to land and she complied. Right away she was beset by the figures and placed in chains.

"Sister, sister, sister, don't you recognize your siblings?" the hooded figure grabbed one of the knights by the neck.

"Please I have a fam..." the figure twisted the man's head till it popped off his body and threw both on the ground. The group laughed as Nyka was gagged and bound by chains more suited to hold a ship's anchor than a woman. Rossen and the other soldiers were tied with simple rope. All 3 were placed on a cart and the pets were abandoned to the elements. A man and a woman were driving the cart pulled by 2 horses. The rest were on their own individual horses, following a road that led south.

"I bet your mind is full of questions. Well, allow me to explain who we are and how you play into all this. He grinned at her and introduced himself.

"I am Ajen your brother. Well, half-brother. My mother was part of an important Yagan family. Our father took a liking to her, as he did to all our mothers before abandoning us like trash."

"We saw you raised like the spoiled brat you are. You were always among the leaders and royalty, completely ignoring us. We were destined to rule Tridom but were cheated out of it by you and him. Her name is Zayna in case you were wondering." Ajen began pointing to his fellow conspirators.

" That is Orel. Your other sister over there is Ida. She doesn't speak much when she's angry, which means she is always silent. And that over there is Zasper. We are the five. Abandoned as children but eager to take what is rightfully ours." The five raised their fists to the air and let out a quick salute.

"Well, I hope that answers all your questions, and why we were able to best you, extremely easily if you ask me."

"I owe her a knife in the leg." Zayna said with a fresh bandage on her thigh.

“Soon we will be done with her sister. Just you wait.” Ajen gave Nyka a quick strike to her head and she was out cold.

In the throne room of the Castillo Morta sat Bazetar. He was slumped in his seat resting his chin on his fisted claw, while deep in thought. Sarre stood to his left and sang in a soft soothing voice. Bazetar growled, then slammed his fist on the throne shooting up to his feet.

“That’s enough!” his yell kicked up the air and dust around Sarre as if it were a windy day.

“I am not here for my own health, you were the one who requested that I sing for you!” she pointed her finger defiantly.

“Watch your tongue mortal…” he leaned over and put his face mere inches from Sarre’s.

“or I will…” the slap resonated throughout the room. Sarre lowered her right hand, which was in pain she hid from Bazetar. His look was one of complete disbelief, here stood a mortal weakling standing up to all his power and fury. He caressed his cheek and lifted a claw stopping the charging Trowcans from killing Sarre. Her breathing became more rapid as the fear began to flood in.

“My lord, I do not know what came over me. I…” he gestured for her to remain quiet. He stood straight again and told the Trowcans in the throne room to leave, even Sarre’s minder. Sarre’s thoughts raced in her head. What was he going to do to her? She backed up to the wall as the Troll king turned to face her.

“Little girl, how were you able to muster the strength to stand up to me? Like a fly charging a spider. It makes no logical sense. I am intrigued, please explain this to me.” He reached over gently and pulled Sarre from her refuge by the hand. She was at a loss for words. She had no idea where the courage came from, all she knew was that she was scared for her life.

"I felt it from the first time I heard you sing, but chose not believe it. You are one of Attel's angels born of flesh and bone. All of your kind are always bringing peace, tranquility, and love to all. It is in your nature. That must be it. It is where you got the courage you just demonstrated. Aside from their peaceful aura they also try to keep you in line and on the righteous path. As angry as I am with the lords above, the angels always showed everyone empathy, regardless of their actions." For the first time since his rebellion, imprisonment and reemergence, the Troll King smiled.

"What is she doing here?" Sadanasia shouted. Bazetar's smile shrank to a grin, as he stood erect still holding Sarre's hand. He turned his head slowly to the right and met the eyes of Sadanasia.

"Hello, my queen, have you met the royal serenader?"

"This filth is my sister! How could you betray me?"

"My queen I assure you that this is the first I hear of this. It is most surprising. I am shocked." Bazetar lightly rested his claw on his chest, feigning concern.

"She is a treacherous little..."

"Still, I see no reason why that would be a factor in terminating her from my service. After all a calm King of all, makes a safe world. Not to mention that her very presence soothes me."

"No! I will not allow it! She is my prisoner! To do with as I see fit!" Sadanasia advanced over to her sister with her pointy nails drawn for attack. Bazetar stood between the women shielding Sarre and growling at his queen.

"She is now under my protection. All hear this! This woman is never to be harmed at all! I forbid it!"

"Yes my king!" shouted a group of Trowcans as Bazetar pointed his finger to Sarre. A stream of light and energy hit Sarre on her forehead and began to envelop her body. Sarre was scared but felt no pain as the light cloaked her in shimmering hexagonal patterns. The new suit soon became invisible and the Troll King lowered his hand.

"I will always protect you from harm my angel." He gave his queen a stern look and then walked away leaving the two women in the throne room by themselves. As soon as he was gone Sadanasia let out a loud angry cry and lunged at her sister. Sarre screamed as her sister's claw came towards her face. The claw struck and bounced off her sister harmlessly as the hexagonal pattern appeared and faded in the area that was hit. Sadanasia continued to strike Sarre many times till her nails began to dull and crack. Sarre was amazed at the fact that the massively powerful hits didn't even move her. She stood back up and just looked at her twin with a slight smile of defiance. Sadanasia was breathing heavily, trembling with rage, and grinding her teeth.

"You. You think this is over?" Sadanasia screamed again and ran to the Trowcans who were standing nearby. One by one she struck them down savagely, ripping them to shreds. She gave her startled sister one more glance and leaped through the enormous window shattering it to a million pieces. The queen unfolded her wing dress and hovered outside the throne room.

"You think you've won? You think you can beat me!" Sadanasia addressed her sister who was now standing at the broken window seeing her twin's gray scaly form now in the sunlight. Sadanasia began to growl, then roar as her nude form began to change. Her size became greater, and her face grew a large snout full of jagged teeth. Sarre could not believe her twin sister was now a flapping monster of a dragon.

"I cannot be beaten!" Sadanasia said in 2 voices, one hers and the other of a massive dragon. She looked to the castle invaders and blew a column of intense fire at them. The soldiers took cover, but the fire was stopped by the orb shield around the upper castle. Sadanasia roared again in immense frustration and flew over to the window into Sarre's chamber. There she shot another column of fire that obliterated Sarre's room along with all her most treasured possessions. There were all the things she had collected over time as well as the gifts given to her by her parents. Sarre just stood by helplessly, watching the pointless destruction. Sadanasia looked to her to make sure she could at least see a tear in her eye. When her lust for hurting her sister was fulfilled, she flew off to another part of the castle.

On a lower tier of the castle many men looked up to the events above. One of them was Abel whose eyes were following the path of destruction from Sarre's chamber to the broken throne room window. There he saw a figure that did not look Trowcan. He pulled out Matiun's old telescope to get a closer look. Instantly he recognized his sister. She was alive and he waved his arms and yelled trying in vain to get her attention. He grabbed a red-hot poker stationed by a brazier nearby and fired one of the cannons brought over from the ships. The report of the cannon echoed through the air and Sarre turned to look at the tiny figures signaling her. It was him, her brother, she just knew it. The tiny figure gestured her to come over and she gave a quick nod in excitement. She ran through the castle past many Trowcans who viewed her with curiosity. Finally the two reached the Orb shield with heavy breath and rampant emotion. Abel was walking to the very edge of the Orb Shield to get as close as he could to his sister.

"Stop right there Abel! He may be able to kill you even with the shield!" Sarre held her palms out. Abel stopped 15ft from the edge. Energy from the shield buzzed and crackled.

"Sarre! My sister you are alive! I'm so glad to see you! Are you hurt? Are you okay?" the prince now surrounded by guards spoke with great concern.

"Yes, I'm fine. I was being held prisoner by our sister but now am in the service of Bazetar." She said in embarrassment as she held both her hands to her chin.

"You don't know how happy it makes me to see you. How is Xenon?"

"Our brother is safe on a heavily fortified ship. It is maintained at the ready to escape in case this incursion fails. Sister, I will find a way to release you from this prison."

"Well, well, well, who is this stunning beauty I have yet to meet?" asked Migus while throwing a cup of wine to the floor.

"Dear sister this is lord Migus of Tridom. He has come to assist in our retaking of Kreshant."

"Well, I see where all the beauty in the Sagen family went to." Migus walked right up to the Orb Shield and placed both palms on it. He felt light zaps and rubbed his hands together to soothe the pain. My lady I assume you are Sarre? I have heard about you." Sarre's brow crinkled in confusion as she took in the admiration.

"Don't you worry my sweet princess; I and I alone will rescue you from that vile creature." Sarre stammered in disbelief and returned her focus to Abel.

"How will you rescue her if you are dead lesser god?" quickly everyone unsheathed their swords and got into attack stances as the 8ft Troll King walked right to the spot where Migus was standing.

"Migus, fallen son of Relo. She is my servant and bound to me in this life and in death. You will not be saving anybody." Bazetar gave Migus his back with his hands held behind him.

"Wow, you're even uglier than I thought." Laughed Migus while looking to Abel's guard for confirmation. Bazetar spun around with immense speed and punched the Orb Shield right at Migus's stomach area. The strike shattered every bone in the god's hand and created a large concussion wave. Outside the Orb Shield it struck outward with such force, that it knocked Migus into the air sending him careening into a castle tower. The lesser god broke through the masonry and disappeared from view. The Troll King winced in pain as he viewed his mangled claw. He made a few movements with it and every bone was set back into place. The claw was fully healed and the burns from the shield flaked off. He then turned to Abel.

"Abel, you are no longer a prince for you have no country, but I am kind and reasonable. If you beg I will make you into a Trowcan regular when I pluck your soul from the Plains of Sorrow. How does that sound?"

"You are a murderous wretch and I along with what remains of my family will have our revenge. Sit tight Bazetar, relish in what little time you have left on the throne." Abel shot a look to Sarre remembering that she was at Bazetar's mercy and stopped his tirade.

"I am eternal. I will always be. Now we must go, say goodbye my serenader." Sarre bowed her head and waved to Abel. With her hands grasped in front of her she followed Bazetar into the castle.

"Sarre I love you and I will free you!" she was gone. Migus rose from the pile of rubble around him. He walked up to Abel rubbing the back of his head.

"You would think a being that old would have learned to take a bit of constructive criticism." The men walked away, each going to their own duty station.

Bazetar continued his walk. He really didn't know where he was going or why he had Sarre following him.

"Why are you so violent?" asked Sarre in an angry voice. Bazetar turned to face her speechless at the question.

"Those are good noble men out there. They have all lost more than most do in a lifetime. Yet they are here to try to vanquish you, a being they know is far more powerful than them. How is all this destruction helping anyone?" Bazetar looked to her with a barely audible growl. She kept looking into his glowing eyes that were beginning to fade. She could even make out light colored pupils.

"The gods need mortals like a business needs its consumers. I was given the task of watching the dead eons ago. As time passed, I felt I wanted more. I wanted to be free. Now, though I no longer hold the position I am still his prisoner. I am still a slave to Attel's will. Bazetar's voice grew deeper, and his eyes turned black. I was once lord of all, my reign was eternal until the cruel Attel arrived from the abyss and attacked me unprovoked." The light around the castle began to dim in pulses. The army outside looked to the sky as the sun went from a bright yellow to a dull orange.

"Our fight lasted for ages but Attel bested me and split my shapeless form in half. As he tried to imprison me, one of my pieces managed to escape. Over the vast distances of time, I have been imprisoned and my other half lost to eternity. Wandering aimlessly as we both wither away." The voice coming from Bazetar's mouth was not his own. It was audibly weeping for itself and controlling his movements. The Troll King began walking to Sarre in sharp jerking movements, his teeth were chattering as it seemed two forces fought to control him.

"We will have our revenge!" the deep voice changed into a high pitch then stopped completely as the glow in his eyes returned and the darkness faded. Bazetar looked at himself asking Sarre what had happened then his eyes widened in horror. She was in his grasp without a sign of life. Bazetar tried frantically to wake her, but she was unresponsive. He let out a thunderous roar of anguish that shook the very walls of the Castillo Morta.

"The former god of the dead ran through the halls looking for a bed suitable for Sarre. Every door he opened violently flew off its hinges as he searched. Finally, he reached the chamber door of Sadanasia. There he saw a large fluffy bed fit for royalty and kept to such standards. He carefully laid her on the bed while talking lightly under his breath saying she would be fine. Once she was situated, he held out his palm and began to blow a blue mist into her nose and face. When she did not respond he continued to do so desperately. The mist soon filled the room and flowed out the open double doors.

"What is she doing here!" Sadanasia, attracted to all the commotion walked into her bedroom chamber.

"Get that thing out of here. Now!" she demanded while pointing at her twin.

"She is in critical danger! I have to save her! She is an angel!" Sadanasia let out a guttural yell and charged the Troll King. She clung to his back and struck it with balled fists.

"I am your queen! You do as I wish. You are nothing but a fool and coward." Bazetar stood, grabbed his queen from the waist with one claw, and threw her out of her room. She landed 5ft from the entrance looking at her king in disbelief as the doors slammed shut on their own.

"You can't do this to me! I am Queen Sadanasia! All bow to me! I am above all! Do you hear me! Above all!" Bazetar stood over Sarre holding her hand and whispering to her.

"You are going to be fine my princess, you're going to be fine." Just as he was losing hope, he saw her chest rise weakly and then with regularity. Sarre took many heavy breathes before she opened her eyes and looked to him. He smiled as a sole tear ran down the black markings of his face.

"I am so glad you are still with me" he pulled her in gently for a hug. Instinctively Sarre lightly returned the embrace. She needed to hold someone after what she had seen. Bazetar felt like this individual was the only thing keeping him going now. His existence held a purpose now, to keep her alive and in good health.

"I saw it." She said weakly

"Who child? Who did you see?" asked Bazetar

"The shapeless one. Part of him is in you and the other..." she began to hyperventilate with fear.

"Calm down princess." He continued to soothe her with his blue mist.

"He showed me things. Horrible, things. If he ever finds his other half." Bazetar stood and looked down at the princess trying to process what he had just been told. He walked to the door unable to hide his look of concern.

"You will stay here till you get better. I will have my Trowcans see to your quick recovery. Good day princess." The doors opened and closed on their own as Bazetar quickly disappeared into the castle.

At a clearing in the forests of the East Shore camped a group of travelers. Three were bound and five were resting for the big day that was coming. Nyka and her companions were still clad in chains while tied to a cart.

"Well hello my sleepy sister. I hope your accommodations are up to par with what you have been grown accustomed to." Ajen and the rest of the five broke out into laughter. Rossen and the other soldier began to move to see what was going on.

"Sister, I am so eager to kill you I can barely think straight." At that moment Zayna raised her arm holding one of Nyka's throwing knives and came down on her thigh. Ajen rushed over and grabbed his sister throwing her to the ground. Nyka yelled in muffled cries as blood rushed out from the blade that was still stuck in her leg.

"What are you? Some kind of idiotic fool?" Ajen scolded Zayna as Ida walked to the princess and pulled out the knife with no care for Nyka's pain.

"All the planning and training we went through, and you would throw it all away this quickly?" Ida held the bloody knife in her hands as she also scolded her half-sister. Nyka's wound slowly began to close reducing the spurts of blood.

"Just stay over there. I apologize sister I just do not know what came over her. Maybe its just your face!" one quick strike hit Nyka in the nose sending her falling backwards on Rossen's thigh.

"Enough, you have proven your point. The princess is helpless." Rossen had worked his gag free and addressed the 5.

"Enough? Enough, you say. Well, what will we do with all this pent up rage then? Simply turn it off. No that is not how it works. We need release." Ajen reached into the cart and pulled out the soldier next to Rossen with ease, holding him by the waist.

"He will do nicely." The soldier began to plead for his life calling out to Rossen for help. Rossen told them to take him instead but he was ignored. Ajen turned to face his siblings.

"Zasper catch!" the soldier was airborne and fell from 20ft in the air. As he plummeted towards Zasper, he removed his hands and let the mortal slam into the ground.

"Whoops, I was never good at catch. Here let's see you Orel!" the still living man had his broken body tossed up again and again till the crunch of broken bones was replaced with the slap of a blob of flesh.

"Well I'm tired how about you my brothers?" all smiled and nodded in agreement. Ajen walked over to Nyka and Rossen with a devilish grin on his face.

"Just think of what awaits you." He held Nyka's chin and began to laugh again. She pulled away and the 5 retired to their tents their bloodlust sated for the moment.

8

"That is so horrible." Said Marci, holding her hand to her mouth.

"How can people be so cruel?" Maya asked her teacher.

"Well children, the 5 were very angry at their father. Years and years of hearing the poison from their mother's mouths made them feel betrayed by Nwendor. Such feelings are very hard to turn off once they take over your soul." The candles began to dim again then return to normal.

"How did the 5 make it to Boe Chantra so easily?" asked Crux.

"No one knows for sure, but the common theory is that they snuck aboard a Sagen ship on the way to attack Kreshant."

"Stosay, do you think the shapeless one still exists?" Stosay remained silent and still. Again, he was lost in thought and the empty voids in his mask stared at the children.

"No, it has been years since these events took place. I for one am glad that all has settled and that there is peace now." The children breathed a sigh of relief as the darkness did not come this time and their cheery teacher continued the lesson.

The Return Of Kragnus

The Trowcan flew fast trying to make it to the Castillo Morta before his army would get there. He was atop a mount that was only reserved for higher level officers as they had to be extremely mobile during battle. Carrying him with flapping wings was a flying wolf. The creature was big, vicious, and was an adept flyer. As he traversed over long distances, the flying wolf began to snarl at something on the ground. Kragnus landed his mount and was greeted by a dragon and giant dog pinned to the ground by ropes and chains. Pykas growled and barked ferociously at the Trowcan who approached slowly.

"Easy dog, I'm here to help." The Battle Hound made quick jerking movements as it snapped at Kragnus. He pulled out his double sword and walked over to Dotoria. She began to struggle more furiously the closer her got to her. She let out a purple ball of fire that Kragnus dodged as it flew by collapsing a nearby tree.

"You are special. I know who you are little lizard of the gods." The little dragon looked into his eye and calmed herself. Kragnus let out a chuckle as he lifted his sword and struck at the dragon's bindings. The flying wolf crawled over with much excitement trying to get a bite of Dotoria.

"Get back!" ordered Kragnus pointing his sword at his mount. The flying wolf retreated, crawling on it forelimbs which were bat-like and walking with it wolf-like rear legs. The Trowcan had a fondness for animals of all types. The fact that he found these 2 out in the lifeless landscape brought him a very small amount of delight.

"I am sorry little lizard, but these chains will be your own to remove. You should be able to get to safety after you crawl out from underneath them." He turned to Pykas and began cutting away at his ropes. The hound growled and barked the whole time. When it came time to cut the last one holding him, Kragnus got a running start, sliced the rope and jumped on his flying wolf with Pykas in hot pursuit. Kragnus just barely made it to the safety of the sky before Pykas caught him. He continued his flight south.

As the Trowcan general continued south he noticed the tell-tale tracks of a cart and horses. He steered his flying wolf away from their intended course to go investigate. As night fell he spotted a campsite from above and landed his wolf a good distance away so it would not be seen. Quietly he snuck over to the area lit by a campfire where he saw a man being thrown up in the air like a ragdoll. He noticed Nyka and Rossen tied to the a and the 5 kidnappers. He had never seen them before but felt their power as well as Nyka's. He would not get any closer to them. He snuck back to his flying wolf after the 5 turned in and flew away into the night. He wondered why there were 5 demi gods holding one hostage. He thought of all the possibilities and came to only one conclusion. An event was about to take place that would create a bit of chaos among the castle defenders. He smiled as he began to contemplate the possibilities.

The next morning Nwendor walked over to main castle wall and rested his arms on the battlements. Matiun walked to him holding a cup of tea to his lips.

"Is all well Lord?"

"My daughter has not returned yet."

"I see, well I am sure she is fine. That girl is extremely gifted in the arts of warfare."

"Which is why I feel she should've been here by now. When I first arrived on Tridom, I conquered my piece of it and then organized an expedition to find my daughter. Her mother was originally from Sukrens. The trek through was long and treacherous because it is a land locked country in the middle of the continent. I lost many loyal Yagan soldiers along the way, but we finally reached the village I destroyed. There was no one there. It was a littered with the bones of the dead inhabitants. I couldn't bare to stay any longer. We continued trekking around the country asking the locals for information and fighting off bandits and the local wildlife. We reached another village that was also void of life. The red plague had arrived and killed everyone. I told my men to stay out so they wouldn't get sick, and I went in. I walked among the piles of putrid dead in the streets for a long time. That is when I heard the cries of a baby coming from one of the houses. I went in and saw the bodies of my in-laws caked in dry blood. My baby girl was still in her basinet wailing in hunger and to be cleaned. I grabbed her and held her for what seemed like days. I cleaned her and fed her milk we purchased at another village. I held her close to me the rest of the way back. The journey back did not seem as long and before we knew it, we were home. I raised her as I saw fit. I taught her what I knew. The servant women taught her what pertains to girls."

"That...was quite a tale. If the princess could survive that, then surely a mere voyage accompanied by armored soldiers will be extremely easy for her. Don't worry my lord, I'm sure she is just fine." Matiun put his hand on Nwendor's shoulder and walked over to the edge of the tower to view the defenses as he had many years before.

"The causeway will have to come down." Marcus walked up to the battlements.

"Once the Trowcans arrive, our weakest point will be there."

"Yes lord Marcus, we have placed barrels of explosive power at the base of every column in case we need..."

"You will need to. What is coming is a far bigger force

than we encountered on Tridom" Matiun bowed his head to Marcus in agreement.

"How long will the orb shield hold?" Matiun asked the lesser gods.

"Attel made it so it is impervious to attack from even the elder gods, but it seems Bazetar is being assisted by another power." Answered Nwendor.

"The shapeless one." Marcus and Nwendor both looked at each other with distress. Matiun stayed silent, studying the lesser gods while he stirred his cup of tea.

"Did you all see that!" yelled Migus, causing Matiun to jump in fright spilling his tea all over himself and the floor.

"Hot!" Matiun yelled in pain trying his best to keep his clothes away from his skin.

"The Troll King punched the orb shield and barely grazed me" He said under his breath "then he made the entire sky turn dark." Migus paused for effect.

"My fellow gods, I think he might be the shapeless one." Migus held his hands out and nodded to Marcus and Nwendor with a big smile. Marcus turned rolling his eyes as Nwendor starred at him with a blank expression.

"Migus, you are a buffoon." Marcus continued to take in the size of the castle and the landscape. His eyes moved towards the empty city of Sagen where noticed a raging fire in the town square. The 3 lesser gods and Matiun looked upon the flames wondering what had caused it. A commotion was heard among the soldiers manning the main castle wall. All of them left their perch and raced down to the gatehouse plaza. The small garrison deployed to patrol the city was returning with many of them injured or missing.

"You there! What has happened?" Marcus pointed at an

injured soldier with a bleeding leg limping into the castle.

"My King, we were attacked by a powerful foe. They cannot be seen!" the broken man limped faster to find medical attention.

"Let's get moving. Send word to Prince Abel, tell him he is in charge while I am gone." Nwendor, Marcus and Migus ran towards the town plaza. Once there, the gods fanned out walking slowly with their senses piqued. The only sound in the air was the fire that was consuming a temple to Attel. The bodies of 50 badly needed Yagan and Sagen soldiers were laying on the paved ground.

"What has happened?" asked Marcus in a soft voice. Nwendor looked around and noticed a person chained to an iron chair in the center of the plaza. His eyes widened when he saw that it was Nyka.

"Nyka!" he shouted as he began to get in his running stance. Ajen appeared from behind her accompanied by his 4 other siblings all dressed in battle gear.

"Friends of yours?" asked Migus already holding his eleven point spear at the ready.

"What are you doing here?" asked Nwendor.

"Well, father, we are here to exact our revenge on you and her. We were never given the royal treatment, or even your fancy finger blades." The blades of Nwendor were not something that was inherited genetically but were a gift from Aires when he created him. They were made from the metal of the weapons belonging to Boe Chantra's greatest warriors. Aires forged them into thin blades and blessed them with incredible sharpness and durability. Nyka was covered with a blanket that Ajen removed swiftly revealing all of Nyka's throwing blades stabbed into various parts of her body. She had them in her legs, abdomen, and chest. Her breathing was labored and she was barely conscious.

"Like mother, like daughter." Said Zayna as she poured a bucket of oil on her half-sister. She also walked over to Rossen who was tied to a log on the floor and poured what was left onto him. Ida placed a pile of oil soaked logs under Nyka's chair. The 5 broke out in laughter while pulling out an assortment of swords.

"Now, here is how we are going to do this. We will set them on fire and you 3 have to best us before they turn to piles of ash. Are we clear?" asked Ajen.

"Young man, there is no need for such violence. Something comes this way and it will kill us all. This is not the time to fight amongst ourselves." Pleaded Marcus in a stern voice.

"We do not care for the coming fight. You will have to deal with that on your own. We will leave here and fortify Tridom as its new and rightful rulers. Save your breath big man. This is going to happen." Ajen lifted the torch he was carrying and threw it to Rossen who promptly became a living pyre. He screamed in agony as the flames consumed him. Nwendor made a motion to assist Rossen but Zayna held a torch over Nyka and gesture, "no" with her finger.

"You three stay right where you are. Brothers, if you please." She pointed to the lesser gods and 4 of the five sprang into action.

Elsewhere Abel franticly assembled a platoon of his best knights that he would lead to assist the kings of Tridom.

"My lord, your place is here. You and your men are no match for their power. What will we do if we lose you?" asked Matiun.

"I know what you say is true, but I have to help. Nyka might be out there and in danger."

"My lord I..." Abel and his men rode off into the plaza without letting the old man finish his sentence. Matiun ordered the castle garrison to remain at the ready. His old legs moved him quickly about the castle walls. After giving a series of orders to various men, he retired into his room. There he went over his charts and maps still hearing the commotion outside. Two guards were stationed at his quarter's entrance and were tasked with his protection. Matiun held a map close to his face with detailed illustrations of the Castillo Morta. A low grunt followed by the sound of spilling liquid was heard outside. He tried to see what caused it when a cloaked figure walked into his quarters.

"Who are you?" the old man asked as he backed away.

"Oh, just a really old friend. My, how the years have lashed at you." Two glowing yellow eyes could be seen as the hood was lowered. The ever present raised lip and sharp teeth greeted Matiun with a smile.

"Kragnus. Is that you? How is it possible after all these years?"

"I was never killed old man. During the battle with you cousin the remainder of the army retreated. I was among them. Eventually they all ended up dead, but not I. I didn't even age. Just my luck I guess." Kragnus stood taller than the old Matiun by 6in. He crept closer walking at a snail's pace till he was right in front of him.

"My lord wishes you dead. He worries your talent for siege defense is something that cannot be over looked. I disagree, the number of obstacles set for the coming horde would never be enough to completely stop it. Eventually your men would become fatigued. That would happen with the first 100 thousand that I throw at you. The other 400,000 would simply be to show off our might." Kragnus began to chuckle.

"Our strategy is... well, there is no strategy. We are simply a wave washing away the useless filth from this land." Kragnus reached for his double sword and held it in a relaxed position.

"Why kill everyone? There is nothing to gain." Matiun asked.

"Oh but you are wrong sir. The living keep the gods in existence through worship. Kill the living, no more gods. That is what Bazetar is after. He is just a pompous, arrogant fool that we all have to deal with. Personally I do not care what happens to him, or you." With one quick thrust Kragnus impaled Matiun with his double sword. The old man looked to his attacker with shock and slowly sank to his knees. He gasped for air as he faded away. Kragnus stared into his eyes with an evil smirk till he was gone. The Trowcan put him on his bed and scurried out the door to his awaiting flying wolf, disappearing into the night sky once again.

The 5 were strong and fast, but lacked the abilities of the lesser gods. Two of Nwendor's children attacked Marcus at the same time. Orel and Ida took swings at him with their swords but were easily swatted away by his immense strength. He made sure not to kill any of them so as not to upset their father.

"You little spoiled brats, get back!" Migus swung the spike balled end of his spear to strike Zasper's head.

"We need to finish this Nwendor, it is your call." Nwendor was only using telekinetic pulses to keep his children at bay while trying to make his way over to Nyka but the attacks kept coming from all sides. Ajen was thrown and he landed next to Nyka. The blades still stuck in her prevented her from healing fully. Ajen stood and grabbed a torch that had been extinguished. He tried to light it with a starter stone when an arrow flew through the air and went into his hand that held the stone. He yelled in pain as 4 more arrows flew into his chest causing him to retreat. Abel ran to Nyka and was horrified by what he saw had been done to her. He was unable to remove the heavy chains but was able to carry her with help from his men to safety.

"She's mine!" yelled Zayla with her sword in hand. She lunged at the men with great speed but was tackled by quick moving figure. She came to her senses and felt great pain like she never felt before in her chest. She saw 4 long thin blades protruding from her chest. Behind her stood her father looking at her with his slit pupils.

"I am sorry my girl." Nwendor took a quick swipe decapitating the young woman. He quickly ran over to Nyka, slicing the links in her chains and plucking the throwing knives from her body.

"Okay, enough games!" Marcus grabbed Orel and cut him in half with one swipe of his sword, throwing the upper half like trash. Zasper tried to sneak up on Migus but was caught with a spear in his gut. Migus powered up and sent intense volts of electricity surging though his body, till it burned up, crumbling to the ground. Ajen emerged from his hiding spot fully recovered and out for blood. The arrows that had impaled him were in a broken pile next to him.

"Father! I will have my revenge!" the young man ran at his father who just stood there with his arms at his side. Ajen, so blinded by rage didn't even notice the column of fire blasting towards him till he was completely engulfed. The son of Nwendor struggled and screamed in pain as the flames continued to devour him. Marcus walked over to him lobbing off his head to end his suffering. The charred corpse fell to the ground as Nwendor turned his head to look away. Only Ida was left. She was cornered by the 3 gods and a platoon of soldiers.

"What will you do daughter?"

"Don't you ever call me that!" Ida screamed to her father before getting to her feet and sprinting into the nearby brush. Nwendor raised his hand signaling the men not to pursue. They abandoned the city and rushed back into the castle. Nyka was nursed back to full health in just a few hours.

"I told you this mission would be dangerous. I almost lost you." Nwendor said to Nyka.

"We were just fine till the 5 arrived. Who would've known they were here and had a plan to kill us." Nyka struggled to sit up.

"Rest my daughter. We are not safe yet. Did you see the northern army?"

"I did father, and it is endless. We will be overwhelmed even if Bazetar is killed." Nwendor looked off to the side considering the possibility of losing. It had not occurred to him. The fact that the biggest army ever assembled was on its way to retake the Castillo Morta and that they are outnumbered by a ridiculous amount was barely sinking in.

"I spoke to the Giants but they are spooked. I don't know if they'll be joining us for this fight."

"Rest my dear. You have done well." He put his hand on her brow and lightly kissed it.

"Commander!" an urgent voice broke the silence of the room.

"Not now!" Nwendor said.

"You're going to want to see this." Nwendor stood and said bye to his daughter. He followed the captain that interrupted to a holding area where they had brought in Altor.

"We found him attempting to take a boat over to the fleet." Altor remained silent trying to come up with an explanation.

"Why Altor? Explain your actions."

"Well, you see... my lord...I am your most loyal..."

"Traitor!" shouted a weak Nyka who was barely able to stand.

"He told us that the men had been taken by Trowcans. He had really been helping the 5 set up a trap for us." She fell to the floor and was helped up by two soldiers.

"No that is not what happened at all. I would never betray my own. You have to believe me." Nwendor had heard enough. He began walking slowly over to Altor who was trying to talk his way out of his situation. Nwendor's pupils became slits as his blades erupted from his finger with great speed.

"No, Nwendor stop! please!" managed to come out of Altor's mouth before being ripped to shreds. His screams were heard throughout the castle.

On the deck of the Chrysalis, the Sagen navy's biggest and most powerful warship, stood the young king Xenon. The 8 year old was looking out on his family's kingdom. At his feet were various toys ranging from wooden horses to wooden swords he used to practice.

"Young master, it is time to come inside. You've been out all day. Your brother will be furious if you catch a malady." Said Greta, the old nurse tasked with his care.

"What is taking them so long? I would've killed the Troll King with my bare hands by now." The boy picked up his practice sword and held it firmly in his grasp.

"They are doing what they can lord. Even with the help of the deities, this menace is much more dangerous than anything ever faced before. Now come inside. I have a nice pot of soup waiting for you." Even though the temperature was moderately warm, the old woman always wore a scarf to shield her cold skin. The young boy ignored his nurse as kept staring at the city of Sagen. The buildings still stood despite the growing fire started by the five. He longed to go there and explore. His parents had never let him leave the palace because they feared for his safety. In the distance he saw a large dust storm growing bigger.

"What is that Ms. Greta?" the old widow squinted her eyes trying to focus on what was causing the enormous cloud. Footsteps were heard approaching the king and his nurse as they stood on the deck.

"Ms. Greta. King Xenon. We have grave news from the Castillo Morta." The captain accompanied by two other officers took a deep breath, then sighed.

"Your great uncle Matiun was discovered dead today in his quarters." Greta gasped and covered her mouth, while Xenon remained motionless with his eyes peeled wide open.

"What happened to him?" asked Greta.

"He was murdered by an assassin who also killed his guards." The captain spoke softly trying not to let Xenon hear. Xenon began walking in shock over to his cabin, tears running down his cheeks.

"I am sorry my King but I fear I have more bad news. The Trowcans... have arrived!" Xenon stopped in his tracks and starred off into space.

The 3 lesser gods stood over Matiun's body in a make shift morgue.

"How could this happen? How is it possible that someone was able to get past all the soldiers we have and land this blow to us?" Nwendor put his hand on Matiun's cold forehead in a sign of affection for the old man. He was still wearing his glassed and looked as though he was simply sleeping.

"We need to be cautious; his assassin could still be among us." Marcus said when suddenly the alarm was sounded. The 3 gods left the old man and scurried up to the main wall. They made it to Abel's position where the prince stood in shock at what he was before him. The mass of armed Trowcans spread to all corners of the city of Sagen. The army of thousands began to wrap itself around the crater of the Castillo Morta. The causeway was full of people trying to enter the castle for safety. Abel noticed a group of heavily armored soldiers with helmets that had different facial expressions on them running up the to the gatehouse. The group of 100 were let into the castle where their commander insisted on speaking to whoever was in charge. He was promptly led up to the tower where Abel and the gods were standing.

"My lord Sagen!" exclaimed the soldier.

"That would be him." Migus pointed with his thumb to Abel while leaning on the battlements and holding his belt.

"We are what is left of the King's Guard of Brethen Paya. We have received word that this castle was retaken and rushed over as quick as we could. Our land was left void of life. We tried to repel the invaders, but they were far too many for us to handle. The resulting panic cost countless lives as our citizens tried to flee the carnage. What little of us made it to the Seaward Mountains managed to survive in hidden cave bunkers. We wish to serve you great one. We will fight and die for you as we did years ago for King Crenon!"

"You are most welcome to partake in this fight but do you plan to fight the Trowcans with those funny looking tubes?" asked Abel.

"I know! I know! They plan to launch wads of spit paper to confuse the enemy! Brilliant if you ask me." Migus laughed elbowing Marcus who was quiet and not amused.

"The leader of the Payan elite force pointed his tube to the air and pulled the trigger at his finger tip. The loud report made nearby troops duck for cover and erased the smile on Migus.

"What is that?" Asked Nwendor.

"With these guns my soldiers and I can pick off the Trowcans from afar as long as we have ammunition. It is like a hand-held cannon."

"Okay soldier you and your men will be tasked with defending the gatehouse. If a wall crumbles, you will be moved there." Commanded Abel.

"As you wish my lord!"

"Your name good sir!" said Abel.

"King Tetso, I am your uncle." And the 100 men left quickly to take their position, leaving Abel with a perplexed look on his face.

"Never a dull moment wouldn't you say?" Migus grabbed his spear and patted Abel on the back.

As the Trowcans began to gather on the rim of the crater, a peculiar thing began to take place. Gathered on the causeway were a group of 1,000 Trowcans who broke ranks and began running down the causeway. The rest of the Trowcans looked upon them with confusion. As they ran towards the gatehouse they waved their arms and held their weapons in rested positions. The fastest Trowcan pulled out a spear with a white flag tied to the spearhead.

"What trickery is this?" asked Abel.

"I will see what is going on." Marcus quickly made his way to the crenulations at the top of the gatehouse and shot a fireball at the feet of the Trowcan with the flag.

"That is far enough Trowcan! You are on very treacherous ground here! What is it that you want? The Trowcan fell to its knees and held his arms out.

"We beg the forgiveness of you and the other gods. We do not want to be damned anymore. We have learned the error of our ways. We just want to be at peace. We will fight for you and

Attel to prove ourselves." The rest spoke in agreement.

"I find it very hard to believe that you are here to help your sworn enemy. Do you take us for fools?"

"My lord we are changed! The veil of confusion and malice has left our eyes. Allow us to hold this plaza for you. We don't even need to be let in the castle!" Nwendor and Migus had just arrived and looked on to the Trowcan defectors. Marcus remained silent as all the eyes of the garrison were upon him.

"You may stay and hold the plaza, but make no mistake in understanding that you will not be let into the castle. Even when you are overrun by you brethren. If you choose to turn on us, you will be dealt with swiftly like all the other Trowcans brought forth to the walls. Understood?" Marcus stared at the Trowcan leader.

"Yes lord, we simply wish to sacrifice ourselves to try to ensure the survival of humanity." The Trowcans were allowed to form a line on the gatehouse plaza and hunkered down for the battle.

"You really think they are here to help us?" asked Abel.

"The funny truth is that the countless souls trapped in the Plains of Sorrow are there of their own accord. If they would see the error of their ways, their souls would shed all their excess baggage and ascend to the realm of Attel." Explained Marcus.

"Is it really that simple?" asked Abel trying to wrap his mind around what he just learned.

"Yes, it is, but the souls down there are immensely stubborn. They believe that they have all been wronged somehow and that they are always right. So they never let the weight of their hubris go, and down there they stay for all eternity. I really do think these Trowcans here have seen the light. There is something in their eyes." Marcus gestured to the 1,000 Trowcans.

The roar of the Northern Army was all around the castle. They were ready to attack, and to fill their bellies with fresh meat. In the distance towards the southeast was an incredible sight. Loud bellows were heard, coming from the mouths of a group of Tugarnas, the giant tortoises of the Diablo Surrians. They stood 500ft tall at the highest point of their carapace, which was cluttered with buildings and houses. The people of Diablo Surr had arrived and brought with them their entire civilization.

"Looks like the vampires kept their word." said Abel leaning over to Migus.

"Yes we did!" everyone looked up at a large gathering of Vampires floating static in the air.

"Ilget! You have returned!" Marcus walked over to where he could address the Vampire that was 20ft in the air.

"Yes lord, we are here to assist in defending the walls. Our position will give us an advantage over the Trowcans." All the vampires were wearing armor and holding bows. Their quivers were filled to capacity with arrows. At their sides were swords for self-protection.

"So gross, I mean just look at their..." Migus pointed and gestured to Abel who only saw a group of well-dressed gentlemen and ladies there to assist them.

"Spread out all around the main wall. An army that size will be coming at us from all directions." Ordered Nwendor.

"Fabulous! You heard the him! To your stations!" the Vampires formed a floating ring above the main wall.

"We are amassing quite a force here. Yaga, Sagen, Trowcan, Surrians, and now vampires. Should be quite interesting." Commented Migus to all.

"Where are the giants?" asked Nwendor.

At the window of Sadanasia's chamber stood Sarre. From her point of view all she could make out was what looked like a grey blanket enveloping everything. She was worried about her brothers and wanted to help, but would never be able to. Still she felt something had to be done. She stormed out of the room, now fully healed, and made her way over to Bazetar. There he sat on his throne with one leg resting on one of the armrests. His chin was resting on his chest and his gaze was blank.

"You have to stop this! I beg you!" she dropped to her knees before him waking him from his deep thoughts.

"What do you know of what is going on Sarre. This has nothing to do with singing. Know the limits of your position."

"I am the Princess Sarre Sagen! I ran this country before you did, and I know that there is no need for the slaughter about to take place here! You can stop this lunacy!"

"Hold your tongue girl! I let things slide with you because of the affection I fell but there are limits to it!"

"No! You are still Bazetar! Scourge of the..." Sadanasia grabbed her sister by the waist and threw her across the floor over 30ft and out the window. Her twin plummeted down hitting the bottom of the Orb Shield. The shield crackled loudly, like a hundred strikes of lightning that rippled about providing a light display for all to view.

"Noooooooo!" Bazetar yelled loudly while standing at the edge of the window and falling to his knees. Sadanasia grinned and touching the fingertips of both of her hands together.

"Now husband, I believe we have a war to win. It would behoove you to begin spawning more Trowcans." The Troll King's emotional pain brought her great pleasure as she jumped out the window taking her dragon form. Bazetar slammed his fist on the throne room floor in anguish. A feeling of intense rage, even more intense than that of his first emergence began to build up in him. He roared in pain as his eyes grew black and the voice of the shapeless one began to seep out of his mouth.

"Come back to me!" the voice cried out from Bazetar's mouth. He stood, holding his arms out as a jet black beam shot out of his chest and into the Orb Shield. The beam kept hitting it in a continuous stream till the Orb Shield began to warp, eventually exploding and disintegrating into the night air. All the forces looked up in unison at where the beam had shot from. Bazetar pointed in sharp snappy movements at the castle defenders and shouted.

"Get them!" the voices of the shapeless one and Bazetar ordered as his arm fell to his side and the Troll King collapsed onto the floor.

9

"Master Stosay, someone is knocking at the front door." Said Crux from the carpet leaning in for a closer look at the window. Stosay slammed his book shut sending dust in all directions.

"You are all released." The students all began to complain in unison.

"You're just getting to the action! Keep going!" ordered Amon.

"I said go!" he pointed to the door with his right hand while holding the book of Boe Chantra's history with the other. The movement of his arm sent a burst of air that extinguished all the candles, leaving the dwelling in the dark. He became jolly again and walked over to the door and opened it. The confused children walked outside even though their parents had not ye arrived to take them home.

"I am Captain Sergue. We are investigators from the royal guard. Can we have a mere moment of your time?"

"Oh I am quite sorry, I am extremely busy at the moment." Two other guards surrounded Stosay keeping him close to the doorway. He looked from side to side at the men who all stood about 3in shorter than him.

"I assure good sir. We will be quick." The children all looked on from a distance at their teacher and talked among themselves.

"Do you know Bethany Helt?" asked Sergue.

"No I do not. I haven't the slightest idea who she is."

"She was one of your students." Stosay began to stammer.

"Um...Oh I see where the problem is here. You see I know her as Little Beth so... I'm sorry I was just a little confused." He chuckled nervously.

"She and her family were found dead in their home. Were you aware of this?"

"I may have picked up on a bit of what the children were saying to each other, but I am unaware of the details. I am so sorry."

"Mr. Tolbar who we already interviewed said that he had already informed you of what happened to them."

"Sorry but a lot of times when people speak to me, I don't hear on account of my horrible disfiguration."

"What does that have to do with..."

"Bye. Bye. Bye. Sorry I couldn't be of more help to you." As Stosay began to walk away, a guard grabbed his arm keeping him from departing. Stosay turned his masked face to the man and growled. The light of day began to dim in pulses as the man felt his obscure muscular frame.

"Let him go." Commanded Sergue. The man eased off his arm and the story sayer walked home.

Stosay returned to his school in shock to find the students were already inside. They sat around crux in a chair who held a book on his laps and held a paper cut out resembling Stosay's mask. The little boy made the other kids laugh with his impersonations of his teacher. The door into the school flew open letting in the bitter cold and putting out the fireplace's warmth. All the students screamed in horror as the imposing figure walked in.

"Am I a joke to you Crux?" The 10 year old trembled as the

mask came closer to his face.

"How you must loathe my teachings."

"No master Stosay."

"Perhaps you and your fellow students are not worth my teachings." He stood tall over the little boy, stuck his hand in his pocket, and began throwing each of them a candy. The class felt a wave of relief and their teacher laughed heartily.

"It was a great impression. Now all of you listen and take your seats while I find the page we were on." The class sat with the noise of wrappers being undone and hard candy bumping against teeth.

"Ah, here we are. The Trowcans finally reached the Castillo Morta. Which on a good day can be seen from here." Stosay pointed to the window.

"Let us begin the final chapter."

The Castillo Morta

"It appears we are up gentlemen." Migus said while looking up at the shield-less castle.

"We need to get up to Bazetar before he starts attacking the men. We also need to form another line of soldiers facing inwards to the upper castle. Who knows how many Trowcans are up there." Abel agreed with Nwendor and sent out the orders.

"Where will you stay Prince?" asked Marcus. I will be all over trying to keep command while you take care of Bazetar. We are all counting on you." Abel was off to man the wall with the men. As the lesser gods ran into the Castillo Morta, a cacophony of 500,000 Trowcan voices were heard taunting the castle defenders. Weapons were being pounded against shields, and anything else that could make rhythmically pounding sound. In unison the Trowcans began their assault. What looked like gray liquid began pouring over the crater rim which was at enough of an incline to allow them to slide hundreds of feet to the base. Once there the Trowcans began an arduous climb over loose rocky terrain to reach the outer wall of the castle. Hundreds were trampled at the bottom of the crater before they could even start ascending. A hail of arrows, cannon fire, and bullet killed them in droves, but they still kept coming. The ones who finally made it to the wall were greeted with boiling water that was poured from massive cauldrons. Thousands of iron grappling hooks attached to chains were thrown to the battlements to allow the Trowcans to scale the wall. The sheer weight of those climbing did not allow for the 3 way hooks to be removed. The causeway was seized by Trowcans who ran all the way across and smashed into their brothers in the gatehouse plaza. They were especially cruel in their methods of dispatching the Trowcan defectors, who kept their word defending the mortals.

The 3 gods ran together ascending the castle in the area once cut off to them by the Orb Shield. They easily dispatched any Trowcan they found along the way. They reached the gateway leading to the upper quarters, with were the dwellings of the royal family, when a roar from the sky stopped them. A giant dragon was flapping overhead going straight for the castle wall defenders. It inhaled and then showered a section of the wall in flames. Many men were incinerated while others flung themselves off the wall to escape the inferno. Marcus and the others ran to the top of a tower where he held up his hand and shot a fireball at the creature to get its attention. The fireball crossed the dragon's snout just missing its face. Sadanasia turned and roared at the gods. She flew over to the top of the round tower hovering above the 3 lesser gods.

"I am Queen Sadanasia! The bringer of your deaths." She shot a stream of flames that the gods who ran and ducked from them.

"Hello Queen... whatever. I am Migus, great King of Tridom and gift to all women, these two uglies are my personal body guard. We have traveled long and far to kill you and your husband. Do you mind coming down from there? It would make things a lot easier for..." a pillar of fire almost engulfed Migus who was able to dodge it just in time.

"What a vile, annoying man! You will pay for your disrespect!" the dragon began to inhale the deepest it could before it unleashed with a blast that engulfed the entire top of the round tower. Marcus made a circular motion with his hands before countering the blast of fire. Migus and Nwendor took cover behind him in the only section that was not scorched by the flames. The attack stopped and surprised the queen who thought they would be nothing but ashen piles. Marcus balled both his fists and looked up at Sadanasia with fire coming out of his eyes.

"Your fire comes from air and glands in your mouth, but mine comes from the source of all fire. I am the son of Yarma, the Fire God! I am Marcus!" he held out both his hands and shot out a column of fire so hot it began to liquefy the surface of the stone masonry underneath it. Sadanasia tried to move out of the way but the fire hit her right in the chest. Her roars of immense pain echoed throughout the battlefield. It changed from that of a Dragon to that of a woman, and she plummeted to the ground.

"Sorry we couldn't stick around and chat. That's the way you do it." Migus slapped Marcus on the arm, and he gave him the weakest grin ever. Nwendor looked to Abel's position and saw a great number of Trowcans had made it to the top of the wall where Sadanasia had attacked.

"We have to help them." He jumped from the lofty tower falling to the halfway point when he extended his blades sticking them into the tower and using the friction to slow his fall. He reached the section of wall being overrun and started killing Trowcans. He was whipped into a frenzy killing all the attackers and using his blades to cut the grappling chains they were using to reach the wall. The men cheered him as he left to go rejoin Marcus and Migus.

Bazetar came to after his struggle to control the shapeless one. He sat up holding his pained head. He stood and looked out the window at the struggle below. It was pure death and chaos. Part of him thought it was beautiful. As he stood and turned he saw her. Sarre was alive and limping over to him.

"My girl! How are you alive?" every step gave her immense pain, but she was on a mission.

"The protective suit you gave me coupled with the work of Attel. He spoke to me Bazetar. You and all the damned will return to the Plains of Sorrow and rot there for all eternity! You have to stop while you still can." Bazetar walked to Sarre letting out a frustrated growl.

"The old fool kept you alive so you could deliver this nonsense? I am Bazetar a being above all the gods. Now I have a battle to win."

"You are not listening! You cannot control the shapeless one. He is corrupting you ever more. You will lose and be engulfed by it." Bazetar's eyes widened from his normal scowl to a look of uncertainty. For the first time since his rebellion against his master he began to think about the consequences of his actions.

"Listen to them; they are all dying by the thousands out there." Bazetar looked down to Sarre gesturing out the window, and then promptly exited the throne room.

Nyka ran around the castle killing any Trowcan she saw. She noticed that the ones inside were not as numerous as they had thought. She wondered why the Troll King would've stopped producing them. A nude limping figure with torn wings came into her sights. It was badly burned and still smoking.

"Stop right there!" she yelled to the creature. It slowly turned around in great pain.

"Who are you who would address the great queen of this castle?" Sadanasia was still holding her injured chest oblivious to her lack of attire.

"I am Nyka, daughter of King Nwendor."

"Daughter of a King you say." Sadanasia began laughing and till she coughed up blood on the floor.

"You are an intruder, nothing more, and will be dealt with as one." He eyes lit up and her lower jaw extended 5 times lower than it normally did. Fire zoomed over to where Nyka was standing causing her to hide behind a support pillar. Sadanasia slowly and painfully transformed once again into her dragon form although this time she could not fly. Nyka stared in awe at the injured beast that was once a woman. With great speed she sprinted over to the queen and plunged her sword into her neck. She held on to the handle pulling the sword downward and slicing open a great bloody wound on Sadanasia. The dragon shrieked in great pain, then its tail swept the floor knocking Nyka on her back. The dragon slammed its front foot on Nykas legs crushing them. Nyka screamed in pain while driving her sword into Sadanasia's forearm. The weakening dragon growled painfully, and extended her neck upwards while taking a deep breath. Flames were reaching out of her neck wound as she tried to build up enough power to end Nyka. Suddenly a stream of fire hit Sadanasia's laceration causing her to open her mouth in an intense explosion. Nyka noticed the color of the flames that saved her. They were purple. Dotoria landed next to her in her full form. She whimpered as she looked over her frail state. Nyka used her arms to climb atop Dotoria crying out every time her legs moved. Once on top she glanced to over to Sadanasia who was back in her normal form and motionless on the floor. She and Dotoria took to the air and made their way to the infirmary.

Out on the castle walls the battle continued in all its ferocity. Many defenders were overrun and thrown into the mass of Trowcans below to be consumed. The royal guard from Brethen Paya fired volley after volley into the Trowcans killing them by the hundreds. They would fire a shot, open the breech of their firearm, load in a cartridge from their satchel and fire again. The bodies of the dead outside the walls were piling up to high enough in some areas to allow the Trowcans to jump to the top. The Trowcan defectors still held their ground and fought their fellow Trowcans furiously. To the Southwest, the Surrians dismounted their Tugarnas with ropes dropped from their carapaces. Soon an army made up of fierce men and women formed a line and charged the Northern Army's flank. Abel could see the action taking place away from the castle and felt a second wind.

Somehow the giant tortoises stepping on the Trowcan soldiers below brought him a bit of joy.

To the north there was a blaring sound from a thunderous low pitch horn. It was the giants of Koglan along with a four legged familiar ally. They also formed into ranks and charged the Trowcans, led by Pykas, from the city side. They wielded tree trunks fashioned into clubs and swung them low from side to side. Hundreds of Trowcans went flying into the air landing hundreds of feet away while the battle hound got to work mauling his enemies. Even with the assistance of the two armies, the pressure on the castle did not seem to ease much. The Yaga and Sagen armies were getting exhausted while trying to repel the endless onslaught. Many of the Vampires had resorted to swooping down and slicing the Trowcans with their swords then returning to the air. Safety there was a mere illusion as many of them had already been killed by javelins, destroying their illusion and revealing their grotesque appearance. Abel's voice grew hoarse from constantly giving commands to keep the army fighting. The report of the cannons stationed on the walls didn't slow down since the battle had commenced. Their tips were now glowing a slight red burning the hands of the loaders who still kept inserting the iron cannonballs. Dotoria landed near Abel where he saw the injured Nyka trying to cling to the dragon's dorsal spikes. He ran over to her as Dotoria shrank to the her normal size.

"Princess! Let me help you." He lifted her in his arms making her wince in pain.

"My legs! They are broken!" he took her to the infirmary where there were hundreds of injured and dying soldiers. The surgeons were frantically moving around trying to help the defenders.

"Just set me down here. I'm starting to feel better. No need in taking the bed of one who needs it more."

"I'm sorry I wasn't there to..."

"Please prince, you would've only succeeded in slowing me down." Abel chuckled and stood to join his men. She held his hand firmly for a moment.

"Thank you." They smiled at each other and he left to continue the fight.

Elsewhere, a lonely charred person dragged herself on the castle floor. She was trying to get somewhere to find help. She was on her belly, digging her nails into the floor and pulling herself forward. Each pull cost her dearly as the pain transmitted to every point of her broken body. Tears flowed from her eyes, splatting of the floor. A pair of heavy footsteps approached her.

"My queen, you are not well." Said Bazetar, while standing over her.

"My king. How glad I am to see you. Quick, help me." She rolled to her side smiling to him revealing her sharp teeth.

"Now why would I ever do that?" his claws were now holding his waist.

"I am your queen. You love me. That is why."

"I am the god of the dead. I love no one except, maybe you twin sister." Her eyes widened and she screamed with rage and agony that was both physical and emotional.

"You will stay there child. I relieve you of your royal position." Bazetar began to walk away leaving the crying, loathsome Sadanasia to her fate. Her rage was gone replaced with a feeling of extreme sorrow for herself and abandonment. She sobbed there on the floor for long time.

"Queen Sadanasia. Why do you despair?" these footsteps made no noise. She turned to look at the familiar voice behind her in the shadows. There he saw the glowing yellow eyes, and the permanent scowl baring the teeth on one side of his mouth.

“Leave me Kragnus.” She continued crying.

“Please my queen let me help you.” He rushed forward gently cradling her arm.

“Don’t you touch me!” she slapped his claw away.

“What happened to you?” he asked

“I was attacked and betrayed! Betrayed by everyone! You’re all against me.” She broke down even more.

“I thought he loved me...”

“My poor queen.” He held her chin to look into his eyes.

“How could anyone ever love you?” she looked into his grinning face as his double sword entered her chest.

“Ever the sniveling little brat you ever were.” There was no roar or growl this time. Simply a soft high pitched whine as the Trowcan general twisted his blade causing unhealable damage. He stepped away back into the shadows, still smiling as her head hit the floor, bouncing once. Queen Sadanasia’s short reign was over and her heavily laden soul was off to meet the judgement dragon, Helgon.

Bazetar walked now feeling aimless. The voice of the shapeless one was filling his mind with thoughts of corruption and darkness. He began to hold his head in confusion while his eyes went from glowing to black constantly. He was on his way to stop the fight, but the shapeless one’s voice would not relent.

“You will let them be slaughtered! We do not need the gods anymore!”

“Leave me be! I am god of the dead!”

“You are simply my temporary vessel. If you will not listen to reason then I will do away with the cause of this foolishness!" his eyes now a dead black, the shapeless one made the Troll King leap back towards the throne room to deal with Sarre. Sarre was resting on the floor when the troll king entered through the broken window.

"Bazetar?" she asked

"No. The shapeless one. You meddle where in affairs not your own and now my vessel is corrupt with you influence. You must be destroyed." Bazetar slowly jerked over to her position battling his possessor. Sarre struggled to get to her feet while holding her bruised rib and tried backing away. Bazetar's eyes signaled the battle for control of his body. The struggle ended with a concussive roar with his arms outstretched. Before he could reach her, his eyes began to glow again as he breathed heavily.

"It is me my girl. I am back in control. I am so sorry my dear. The battle ends now. We will have peace." He walked to Sarre who was smiling at him awash with relief that the war was going to finally end. From the rafters of the throne room shouted a voice.

"Bazetar! Your rule is over!" Marcus leaped from his perch, summersaulted once, fell 40ft, and landed on the Troll King. He was impaled through the base of his throat and out the base of his spine with Sun Piercer. Marcus extended both arms with his palms aimed at Bazetar's torso and hit him with a blast of scorching fire. Bazetar was pushed backwards all to way to a support column where he still struggled with the sword in his body. Bazetar grabbed the blade as it stuck out of him and pulled it all the way through, hilt, handle and all. Marcus barely had time to duck as the sword was thrown back to him getting stuck in the support column behind him. The huge hole in his torso closed quickly as he began walking towards Marcus.

"Stop both of you! There is no need to..." pleaded Sarre.

Nwendor lunged at the Troll King in a diagonal blade first descent. His blades pierced Bazetar's chest exiting his back. The Troll King grabbed Nwendor with one hand and slammed him once one a pillar, once on the floor, then threw him to a wall.

"If you want to continue as enemies then by all means lets..." a bolt of lightning struck Bazetar in the face sending his body into convolutions. He lifted a claw and responded with a heavy burst of energy that hit Migus and blew a hole in the roof above. Migus picked himself off the floor while supporting himself with his spear. He turned to Sarre and sprinted over while Marcus and Nwendor teamed up on the Troll King.

"Princess, we need to get you out of here." He tried to pull her towards the doorway.

"No! this needs to stop! He is not the enemy!"

"Oh no princess, he has corrupted you. He won't be around much longer." Migus became furious as he left her side, not hearing her frantic pleas as he charged the Troll King. Bazetar was holding Marcus's shoulder and hitting him with blows so massive, the concussion of them cracked windows in close proximity to the throne room. Suddenly the 11-point spearhead exited one of his eyes and he fell to the ground. Migus gave Marcus a hand lifting him to his feet.

"I have to say, that this has been a very exhilarating exper..." Bazetar stood, backhanding Migus away then uppercutting Marcus, and finally focusing on Nwendor. Nwendor pushed him away with a telekinetic blast, opening him up to a blade attack. One swipe removed his right hand before he to was hit with a blast of black energy. Bazetar roared in pain as he grabbed his severed hand allowing the muscles and tendons to reattach themselves. Once he was whole again he bared his teeth and his eyes began to darken.

"Enough from the likes of you. He held his arms out

and let the shapeless one take full control. The night began to darken even more as the stars, torches, and moons all began to fade. Outside the fighting ceased temporarily because the forces couldn't see each other.

"Now the giants will have a challenge on their hands." Bazetar began to float while looking to the sky. The giants were beginning to make a dent in the Trowcan ranks along with Pykas when suddenly they began to hear a cracking sound. The light returned in pulses to reveal the Mountain Golem coming to life. The behemoth reared his arms back and threw Bazetar's mountain prison with ease producing an earthquake felt by all. The massive stone man walked over to the giants and Pykas where it began its assault. The titan pounded down with its fists crushing the giant warriors under it and trampling the wounded as it walked. Pykas, significantly smaller than all those fighting, ran to escape the fray. The light began to return and the fighting continued. With the giants occupied the Trowcans began to regroup and push back the Surrians. They even managed to climb up and destroy one of the villages atop one of the Tugarnas. The inhabitants were massacred and the structures set ablaze. The Tugarna panicked trampling all, even some Surrians before the heat from its burning shell overcame it, killing it.

Nwendor jumped through the air trying to attack the god but he was shot with a bolt of black energy.

"What are you orders great commander?" shouted Migus as Nwendor was still recovering from his fall. They hid behind the relative safety of the support columns of the roof so as not to get zapped by the constant black bolts. Sarre emerged from her cover and began walking towards the floating Bazetar. His black eyes looked down to her.

"Ah, the meddler. You are too late. I have been given full control of this body. Soon I will emerge on this plain once again." Sarre continued walking towards him defiantly.

"I know you're in there. Ah!" she screamed as a bolt of black energy struck close to her leg.

"Fight it. It wants nothing more than to undo everything and everyone. You can stop him!"

"You are a fool woman; I have had enough of you." Bazetar's body began to transition from smooth fluid motion to sharp jerking movements. The hulking body fell to the ground and his eyes began flashing from black to a glowing white.

"I can't hold him much longer. You have to finish it!" Bazetar pleaded to the lesser gods.

"It is lodged in my beating heart, you must destroy it!" Bazetar laid on his back and dug his own claws into his sternum. One quick pull from both hands opened his chest cavity. There his heart was revealed, beating wildly surrounded by the black goo that was the shapeless one.

"Stay back lesser gods, he is mine you cannot save him!" Bazetar held his bloody chest open but his muscles and bones began to rejoin attempting to close the opening. Bazetar's grip was fading fast but Nwendor jumped on top of him and cut the reparations. He then pulled the ribs father apart revealing the infected heart.

"Now! Do it now!" Marcus and Migus stood at Nwendor's side each sending a thin concentrated beam of fire and lightning into the now agitated mass of muscle. Bazetar's head slowly fell limp with his jagged toothed mouth hanging open. His arms fell lifeless to his sides. His heart began to expand, full of three forces at odds with each other. Electricity, fire, and black energy filled the cramped space till it could hold no more and set off a mighty explosion that sent fragments of the throne room in all directions. The sun began to rise slowly, illuminating the world around all the combatants. The Mountain Golem froze in its place and fell over lifeless. The Trowcan army felt in their guts that something had changed. Their leader was gone, and this time, it was for good. Slowly, the northern army began to back away from the defenders and released their hold on the ground they had won over the night. There was an eerie silence about. Only the breeze and the fires were making any sound.

Marcus removed some rubble that was pinning him down and stood up. Migus ran over to Sarre, her hexagonal shield fading away from view.

"Well princess, that is new." They both turned to look at Nwendor who was standing still over the slain Bazetar. His back was to all of them and they began to hear a noise that was foreign to them. The lesser god was chuckling. Their eyes widened as he erupted in maniacal laughter. He turned to face them as the dust cleared with his arms covered in the black goo of the shapeless one.

"You won't believe it. The power! It is amazing!" he began to rise in the air as Bazetar did earlier.

"Watch as I save us all!" he shouted upwards in his and the shapeless one's voice. His telekinesis was amplified a million fold. With a mere thought all the Trowcan Northern army had their weapons snatched from their hands to where they hovered in the air in front of them. Nwendor's black eyes looked at his audience with his arms outstretched.

"Now to the world's salvation." Another thought exited his mind and all the hovering weapons began to cut down the Trowcans, even what was left of the defectors. The agonized screams of the dying filled the air.

"They will all die! I am the savior of all!"

"Stop Nwendor! Before you're too far gone!" Marcus called out amidst bolts of black energy beginning to emit from his body. The cries of death ceased and all the Trowcans in the northern army and everywhere else on the continent were dead.

Bazetar and his ferocious hordes were no more.

"Stop? Why would I stop? I have saved everyone. Why you ungrateful little swines! I see that you do not all appreciate what I have done for you." the sky grew dark and the sun lost its radiance.

"See what happens to those who do not appreciate their new supreme god!" suddenly all the weapons of the defenders left their hands and floated in front of them. It also happened to everyone around the continent that had survived the Trowcan onslaught.

"Now I will finally be able to find my other half with the world void of all life!" the voice of the shapeless one left Nwendor's smiling mouth.

"We have to do something!" yelled Migus to Marcus. Using his god strength to resist Nwendor telekinetic pull he aimed his 11point spear and flung it through the air at the unsuspecting lesser god. Nwendor grunted looking down at the spear impaling him through the heart. Marcus focused a beam of concentrated fire that hit where the spear was lodged penetrating his chest and exiting the other side. Nwendor fell to the floor. The shapeless one fell off his arms shrieking as it seeped through the floor, disappearing into the masonry. Marcus, Migus, and Sarre hurried over to the fading lesser god as he stared off into space, the life draining from his eyes. He saw a bright light filling his field of view as an angelic hand reached out to him. A very familiar face smiled at him and told him she had been waiting for him.

"Is he smiling?" asked Migus. Sarre grasped her hands together covering her mouth.

"He has found his wife." Said Marcus.

10

"And so, it was my students, that the ultimate sacrifice of Nwendor brought peace and prosperity to the land once again. His soul, now lighter than a feather, was allowed the comfort of his long lost love in the realm of Attel. Migus and Marcus stepped down as kings of Tridom allowing the banished Wrell family to return to the Yaga as their rightful rulers under the condition that the Yaga remain free. Marcus ever the strong and silent god he was, simply returned to his home to spend his days as a father and husband. Migus, remained with the Sagens, now having taken a fancy to Princess Sarre, he was given the title of god protector of Kreshant. He spent his time, not chasing women but bettering the country's defenses and trying to tear down Sarre's. Nyka and Abel eventually married and started a family of their own. They had a set of twins, boy and girl, named after her parents. Funerals were held for both Nwendor and Matiun as well as the countless defenders of humanity. The Yagan army was honored in Kreshant for their bravery and sacrifice to a country that wasn't even their own. Xenon was crowned King of Kreshant. He grew into a young man who had a knack for governing just like his father and grandfather before him. The Castillo Morta was rebuilt and restored to its former glory. There is word that even Bazetar was allowed to enter Attel's realm after his selfless acts. The vampires fled from the battlefield in a display of cowardice when the fighting got too intense. They returned to Montania where it is thought they still reside but there have been no reports. The Diablo Surrians took over the neighboring island of Diablo, which was completely vacant after the Trowcans were killed, effectively uniting them into one nation simply called Diab. The giants who suffered great losses, returned to their lands and shut their gates once again, returning to a state of isolationism. King Tetso returned to the country of Brethen Paya with what was left of his guard and a few other survivors to restart the kingdom. The Trowcan defectors went before Helgon and watched their brethren plummet to the Plains of Sorrow while they shed their heavy hubris and lived on with the gods. The continent was completely devastated, but with time and gifts from the gods, the population of animals and people were restored. The lands were back to their prosperous selves. All remained good because good was all that remained." Stosay closed his book on the history of Boe Chantra while the kids stared at him.

"What a sad story." Said Marci

"No, it wasn't, the action was fun to listen to, especially when they described all the blood and guts." Crux said while simulating a disemboweled Trowcan. The class started to become rowdy and Stosay simply lifted one of his thick mittens to get them settled down. The children's parents knocked on the door and left with their sons and daughters. Stosay closed the door to the school and retreated by the fireplace to tidy up before the next class. The following morning, they would be learning math. As he began setting math books as well as paper and pencils, he heard a voice.

"Master Stosay, you are coming with us." Ordered commander Sergue. Stosay remained as still as a statue as the other two guards emerged from hiding.

"The day we interviewed you, you left in such a hurry that your door was left unlocked. So, we entered your school and found this." He held out a black outfit stained with copious amounts of blood.

"Seems a little small for your frame story sayer, but we'll figure it out."

"He means you are too fat to wear normal clothes." Said

the guard that had detained him by the arm. Stosay remained absolutely still, but the audible growl returned and the school candles began to pulse. Without warning Stosay moved with inhuman speed to a guard hitting him hard over the head caving it into his chest. The guard who had grabbed him unsheathed his sword and wasn't able to see Stosay's mitt reach for his bottom jaw before ripping it off. Sergue tried to swing his sword at him but he stopped his arm in mid swing and punched a hole through his torso. Stosay viewed the carnage while flicking the blood off his mitten, unworried over the sounds made by the men. The place was a mess, but he would have it immaculately clean in no time. He kicked Sergue away from the base of his chair and took a seat. He took in relaxing breaths as the lights regained their brilliance. He used one hand to remove one of his mitts, then he used the free claw to expose the other. One of his three fingered claws reached up to undo the blood splattered mask her wore. With the smiling mask came the long hair that ran down his entire back. A lengthy sigh came out of the raised upper lip of Kragnus as his piercing yellow eyes stared off into the distance.

A Little About The Author

I was raised in a small Texas town on the U.S.-Mexico border. My elementary years were spent being harassed for loving to draw. I preferred getting reprimanded for not finishing an assignment rather than not complete one of my drawings.

I was a fairly average student till I reached middle school. There I began my lost years. What I mean by lost is that I had no idea what I wanted to do with the rest of my life. My grades dropped so low they considered kicking me out of school and I was constantly berated by my parents and just about everyone else to get my act together. I don't understand to this day what happened to make me not care. This pretty much continued till my junior year in high school. Something seemed to just snap into place, and I decided I was going to get my act together.

My grades went up, I had a good set of friends and my parents let up a bit. After graduation I was shipped off to the world's finest navy. There, I performed my duties as were expected of me, toured the continents of Asia and Australia, but I was never happy there. I decided college was the way to go and I was going to be the first in my family to get a degree.

After 4 years active duty, and an honorable discharge, I went back to my Rio Grande Valley home and attended the local university. This began another academic downward spiral as I still had no idea what I really wanted to go for so, had no drive to excel academically. I met my wife, had my kids, bought a house, and dogs but still was at a loss.

I worked many different jobs since the Montgomery G.I. bill helped pay for the training. I was a class A CDL driver, mechanic, and CSR at various call centers. During this time is where

I decided to dedicate myself to the one thing, I was ever any good at. I began doing artworks as well as developing this story I began to think up when I was in 8th grade.

I had made an attempt to make the story into a comic, but the process was too long, and I lacked many of the needed resources to achieve that goal. Now it is finally here, a story that I have always wanted to tell. I used to tell this story to my little cousins Marcos and Miguel when we were kids. We would play the 3 lesser gods in the backyard of my grandfather's store. I had the story drawn out on writing paper in a red binder that has been lost to time. I would show them the stick figure drawing and one time we even recorded ourselves doing the voices on a tape recorder. Sadly, the tape recorder was also lost when my father lost his house. My two cousins, now adults, don't really remember these times, just that we used to play together on weekends.

My wife, Betty's, influence was the main reason I was finally able to get to this point. I can say without a doubt that she is the only one that has ever really believed in me. Without her constant encouragement I would've just left this story to rot and fester in the Plains of Sorrow.

www.ingramcontent.com/pod-product-compliance
Lightning Source LLC
LaVergne TN
LVHW091317150826
845673LV00006B/1678

* 9 7 9 8 4 9 4 6 9 1 1 2 5 *